Lost in Love

Lost in Love

Book Two of Dangers in Love Series

Ana Denise

SIGN UP FOR MY AUTHOR NEWSLETTER

Be the first to learn about Ana Denise's new releases and receive exclusive content!

www.authoranadenise.com

Chapter One

Destiny

"I have a caramel macchiato," the barista called out.

She sat my drink on the counter.

"That's mine."

Approaching the counter, I grabbed the drink.

The barista gasped. She placed her hand over her heart.

"That is one beautiful ring," she commented.

I stared at the white-gold band with an oval-shaped diamond on my finger.

It was a beautiful ring. I had it on for the past nine months. The ring never left my finger, no matter what activity I participated in. I still couldn't believe how I ended up with the wonderful man who gave it to me.

"Thank you."

I took a tentative sip. It was nothing short of perfect.

"I have a vanilla cappuccino."

"That's mine," Zach, my fiancé, called out as he held his hand up.

When he approached the counter, he placed his hand on my side.

The barista looked back and forth between the two of us. She beamed.

"I hope you two have a wonderful day."

"Same to you," I replied.

Turning around, I spotted an empty table on the patio. We walked outside and sat across from each other.

It was a beautiful Thursday morning. It was the middle of spring. The sun shined brightly in the sky. The temperature was perfect.

Zach sipped his drink before he sat back and smiled.

"Is it good?" I asked.

He nodded.

"It's great. How is yours?"

I sipped my drink.

"It's delicious."

Crossing my legs, I clasped my hands.

Once a week, through our busy work schedules, we'd choose one of the days to meet up for a morning drink and chat.

"You have no idea how much I look forward to our coffee dates," Zach said.

He reached across the table and placed his hand on mine. He rubbed the back of my hand, giving me the affection he spoiled me with daily.

"It's the highlight of my morning," I commented.

He squeezed my hand.

"You see me every morning, though," he pointed out.

He flashed me his beautiful smile.

"You see me every night as well."

His statement was valid. We went to sleep together, woke up together, and got ready together. We even headed out the door together.

"It's safe to say I might be obsessed," I admitted.

Zach smirked.

"Are you sure it's appropriate to add might into the equation?"

Looking over the rim of my cup, I sipped my drink. Zach treated me with such delicate gloves while he protected me. Those acts hadn't changed since we left his cabin two years ago, either.

"No. Not at all."

I smiled before I looked at the table. To this day, butterflies fluttered in my stomach. I loved how he still had that effect on me.

"Look at me."

I looked at him. His beautiful brown eyes zeroed in on me. Those were the only eyes that had the power to see deep into my soul.

"I didn't propose to you for no reason."

He cupped my face with his hands. He kissed my chin softly, sending a shiver up my spine. He kissed my nose, and I beamed. My nose was my least favorite physical attribute. Yet, Zach showed it so much care. Finally, he kissed my lips. At the end of the kiss, his tongue snaked out and briefly darted into my mouth.

"I'm in love with you."

He paused, giving me a second to gather myself. Boy, did I need that second. The effect he had on me was nothing short of powerful.

"It's safe to say I've been obsessed with you."

Zach proposed to me nine months ago. He put so much thought into how he would do it. He proposed when it was just the two of us. I couldn't have asked for a better proposal.

"Is it a good obsession or a bad obsession?"

He rubbed his nose against mine.

"Whatever obsession you want it to be," he answered.

I bit the corner of my lip. If we weren't in public right now, the things that would happen...

"You better stop," I answered.

Sitting back, I admired him. He wore a dark purple short-sleeved dress shirt and black slacks. Zach was irresistible.

"What if I don't want to?"

He sipped his drink.

Before I could respond, Zach's phone sounded. He looked at it and exhaled.

"I'm sorry, but I'm going to have to cut our time short."

Ugh.

I hated it when this happened. It didn't happen often, though, so I had to be grateful for that.

"Why? What's going on?"

"I have a meeting to attend in thirty minutes."

Just when the conversation got juicy, it had to come to an end.

Zach and his meetings. They were more plentiful now than they used to be, since his position had changed.

Zach was no longer a lead detective. After Candace's case was settled, he decided it was best to leave the detective work alone for my sanity, so he applied for the assistant chief position. To no surprise, he was promoted. He had been in his new position for six months. It was different from what he was used to, but he loved it.

If you love your job, you'll never work another day in your life.

That's why I loved my job. I still worked as an elementary school teacher. I no longer taught first grade. When I went into protective custody, they hired another woman to take over my class. At first, I wasn't happy. I was only gone for three months. I didn't think they had a right to replace me, but the administration did what was best for my students. The woman they hired to take over my class did a wonderful job finishing off the second half of the year.

I was now a second-grade teacher. Some of my first-grade students ended up being my second-graders last year. Seeing the excitement on their faces when they realized I was their teacher was so nice. I couldn't comprehend how they would be going to third grade in less than two months.

"Good luck with your meeting, sweetie. Don't forget, we have to attend a showing today at five o'clock."

We were on the market for a bigger house. We wanted to upgrade to a three-bedroom house, and it was the perfect time to buy. Prices and interest rates were manageable.

He kissed my forehead.

"I promise I won't miss the open house."

He grabbed his drink and sipped it.

"I'll see you later."

He walked to his truck. My eyes never left him until he left the parking lot.

In less than a week, I would walk down the aisle and marry the love of my life in front of our family and friends. It took nine months to plan the most perfect wedding. Thankfully, I had my mother, my future mother-in-law and my friend, Hannah, offer as much assistance as possible. When the day of the wedding arrived, I knew all the hard work, sweat, and tears would pay off.

A text vibrated my phone.

Hannah: Good morning, sunshine. Only five days left until the big day.

Me: Good morning, Han. Only one hundred and twenty hours to go. I'm not pulling my hair out in chunks, you are.

After I finished my drink, I tossed my cup in the trash and walked to my car.

Hannah: Haha. Will I see you soon?

Me: Be there in ten.

Hannah and I met at Jake's and Emma's house right after Zach and I came back to Sacramento. We were invited to a spring cookout on a beautiful, sunny day.

"Zach. Destiny. You two have made it."

Emma walked out of the house carrying a tray of cut-up fruit. She sat the tray on the food table before she walked towards us.

Emma wore a beautiful, flowy yellow sundress that stopped right below her knees, her hair pulled back into a high ponytail. She towered over me by a few inches.

This was the second time I'd been around Zach's best friend and his family. They were all sweet and welcoming.

"Yes, we wouldn't miss this cookout," I commented.

Even though we hadn't been back in town a full week, it was time for us to get our life back on track.

She pulled me into a hug before she hugged Zach.

"Where's Jake?" Zach asked.

She motioned towards the house.

"He's getting the burgers ready."

Zach wrapped his arm around my waist.

"Can I go inside?"

I smiled. His desire to make sure that I'd be okay without him around me for a few minutes excited me.

"Of course."

He kissed my forehead before he excused himself and walked inside.

"He's a great man," Emma commented.

I couldn't help but agree.

"Yes, he is. I'm not sure what I did to deserve him."

Emma clasped her hands together. She placed her hand on my shoulder and said, "You showed him what genuine love entailed. Nobody else had been given that chance."

She grabbed my hand and walked me towards the corn hole game.

"I'd like to introduce you to my friend, Hannah."

Hannah played a game of corn hole with Aiden and Jayden, Jake's and Emma's six-year-old twin boys.

Hannah tossed her last bean bag straight into the goal before she did a victory dance.

"Aww, not fair," one of the twins commented to the other twin.

They were identical, so it would take me time to tell them apart.

"Hannah, this is Destiny. Destiny, this is Hannah."

Nobody could ever replace the friendship I had with Candace. Nobody tried after learning how my best friend was taken from this world. The friendship I developed with Hannah during that cookout came pretty darn close, though. Especially after we learned that we worked at the same elementary school.

Once I parked in the staff's parking lot, I grabbed my purse and headed into the grand, two-story building. I held the door open for a coworker before I made a beeline for the teacher's lounge.

There were about ten minutes before the bell of the day would ring. Before I gave my attention to my children, I had to see my friend.

I walked into the teacher's lounge. There was a full-size fridge and a microwave, three tables surrounded by chairs that offered little to no comfort, and two sofa couches. Along with Hannah, there were two other teachers present.

"There's the bride-to-be."

Hannah sat on the sofa couch, cradling a cup in her hands.

"I've arrived."

Walking over to where she sat, Hannah patted the couch cushion beside her. She sat her coffee cup on the coffee table in front of her before she wrapped her arms around me, and we hugged.

Hannah taught fourth grade. She arrived

shortly after I went into protective custody to take over Mrs. Bell's class, who went on maternity leave and decided not to come back.

"How are you doing this morning?"

"I'm good. Zach and I had a coffee date this morning at Meg's."

Hannah smiled. "You two never skip your morning coffee dates, do you?"

I shook my head. "Never. They are cut short sometimes, like this morning."

Hannah scrunched up her face before she sipped her drink.

"He had a last-minute meeting?"

"It seems like they come more often than not."

"It comes with the job territory."

"Enough about my love life." Crossing my legs, I sat back, getting comfortable. "How was your date last night?"

Hannah moved to California from Texas after her long-term relationship with her boyfriend ended. She wanted a change of scenery and a fresh start, so she left the Lone Star State and moved to the Golden State. Six months ago, she finally felt ready to dive back into the dating world. She was on two dating apps.

Hannah rubbed her finger under her nose before she shrugged and grabbed her cup.

"It was okay."

Hannah couldn't lie to me to save her life.

I gave her a pointed look. "Why are you lying?"

Hannah smirked. "Fine, it was terrible. The worst date I've ever been on."

I swatted her arm. "Give me the details. I want to know everything."

"He showed up fifteen minutes late, burped after chugging his root beer, and picked his teeth at the table after he swallowed his dinner in record speed."

Hannah touched her index finger to her opposite hand fingers as she listed off all the things that went wrong.

Yikes.

"I can't believe you tried to say the date was okay." I laughed. "What you explained to me sounds like the most disastrous date ever. It won't be a second date, will it?"

Hannah threw her head back and laughed.

"Oh, God no."

She sipped her coffee.

"That might've been the one date that stops me from searching for love."

"I'm afraid you aren't getting out of the dating pool that easy," I commented.

"You weren't even in the dating pool, and you found the man of your dreams," Hannah observed. "Maybe I can have the same fate."

Zach and my love story was one of a kind. We fell in love in the most unconventional and unorthodox manner. If someone had told me two years ago that I'd fall in love in the manner that I had, I wouldn't have believed them.

"Don't let one bad date ruin your outlook on

dating. Trust me, the right man will come along when you least expect it."

Hannah grasped my hand and squeezed it. "I guess I'm going solo to your wedding."

Hannah coming to my wedding by herself was the least of my worries.

"As long as you're there, I don't care who comes with you."

"You know I wouldn't miss your big day." Hannah smirked. "Even if I woke up with a big ass pimple on my nose, I'm still coming."

One thing I could say, Hannah always showed up for me. I didn't have anybody else to thank for our relationship except for Emma.

Checking the time, we had three minutes until the first bell of the day would ring.

I stood, ready to head for my classroom on the other side of the school.

"I have to get to class. I'll see you at lunch?"

"You'll see me at lunch."

We blew air kisses at each other before I walked out of the teacher's lounge and headed for my class.

Normalcy is what I craved. I thanked the Heavens above every day for giving me my normalcy back.

Chapter Two

Destiny

The harmony serenaded my ears. That was my cue. My hands were clammy, and I clutched my bouquet tighter. My nerves were getting the best of me.

"You look amazing, honey bun."

I beamed at Robert.

"Thank you."

I wouldn't want anyone else to stand beside me on this special day.

Our special day.

Taking a tentative step forward, the click of my heels rang out. The silky, smooth fabric of my wedding dress brushed against my legs. I was several feet away from making my grand entrance.

I stopped in my tracks.

Was I ready for this?

"You can do it."

He was right. I could do it.

The doors in front of us opened. Goosebumps rose on my arms as my eyes landed on my fiancé. My future husband. Zachary Henry Miller.

He stood tall at the altar. He wore a black suit accented by a champagne-colored shirt and tie. Shiny, black dress shoes housed his feet. He winked and smiled before he nervously looked away and wiped his eyes.

All at once, our family and friends rose from their seats. All eyes in the room were on me. I was the center of attention. It was my day.

Smiling at our family and friends, I narrowed my peripheral vision to Zach. He was my focus.

Robert and I walked down the aisle as the beautiful melody flowed from the speakers.

The last two years of my life flashed right before my eyes. Great and horrible things had happened. My best friend passed away from gun violence. While finding my best friend's killer, I gained a boyfriend, fiancé, and future husband. I reunited with my birth father. Hannah came into my life and made it a little more bearable. My parents still lived in Florida, but they have visited more often since the case was settled.

Now it was time for me to become Mrs. Miller.

Zach stood only mere steps away from me. After he wiped his eyes with his handkerchief, he clasped his hands together.

We approached Zach.

"Who gives this woman to be married to this man?"

"I do."

Robert handed me over to Zach. A tear escaped my eyes.

As a little girl, I always imagined a fairytale wedding. I just never knew the day would come so quickly.

Zach and I walked up to the officiant.

"You may now be seated," the officiant called out.

Everyone sat in unison. Glancing over my shoulder, I looked at the front row. Robert sat with Mom. Zach's mom, Eleanor, sat with her boyfriend, Benson. Dennis, my birth father, sat beside his longtime girlfriend, Ashley.

I was grateful Dennis came back into my life two years ago, but it was only right for Robert to do the honor of walking me down the aisle. He raised me as his own. He was the man I grew up calling my father. He deserved that honor.

The officiant opened the black leather book in his hands and started the ceremony. Zach and I held each other's gaze as the officiant spoke.

Staring into his eyes, I saw the love he held for me deep within his heart and soul.

"The couple has decided to say their own vows."

The officiant motioned for Zach to begin.

Zach released my hands and dug into his jacket pocket. He pulled out a piece of paper. The paper unfolded, and the paper made its way to the ground.

Laughter vibrated through the room. Zach knew how to bring laughter to a serious occasion.

Zach locked eyes with me before he looked at his paper.

"You're the sunshine of my world. For the longest, I had given up on love. I didn't think love was real. I thought it was something only people experienced in fairytales."

Zach paused. He looked at me, and a salty tear escaped his eye. Reaching up, I wiped it away. There was no doubt in my mind that this day would be full of emotions.

"I didn't know what love was until you showed up in my life. I have you to thank for showing me what it's like to be truly loved. For that, I want to spend the rest of my life with you."

Zach's words. They were so beautiful. How could I compete with that?

"You're my breath of fresh air."

I took a deep breath, willing myself to continue without being choked up. I knew my vows by heart. Tears burned the back of my eyes. I fanned my eyes so my tears wouldn't ruin my makeup that took over an hour to apply.

"You're the reason that I breathe. I never knew what love was until you came into my life. Nobody I've ever met had ever made me question what the possibility of love would be like… until you came along. You showed me what it was like to be cared for. You showed me what it was like to be cherished. I can't wait to spend the rest of my life with you. Through sickness and health, I'll be by your side. I'll be by your side until your very last breath."

A chorus of *ohhh* and *aww* echoed.

"There's nothing left to say after those beautiful words."

The officiant closed the book he held.

"I now pronounce you man and wife. Zachary, you may now kiss the bride."

Zach's bright eyes widened. Zach looped his arm around my waist, closing the short distance between us. He pulled me into his firm chest and grabbed my chin. Our lips met, and an eruption of applause and cheers filled the room.

A smile peeked through the kiss. We pressed our foreheads together before we made eye contact, the first eye contact as husband and wife.

"You're my wife," he said, just loud enough for me to hear him.

"You're my husband."

He kissed my nose before we turned to face our friends and family. As our exit song came on, we walked down the aisle. We waved and smiled at all our loved ones before we made our way out of the tent.

It was a beautiful day at the end of spring, the most perfect day to get married. The sun shined bright in the sky. The temperature was bearable, far from scorching. Walking towards the fountain, our photographer followed close behind, snapping pictures of us the entire time.

As cocktail hour started for our guests, we posed for pictures. We took so many pictures in different poses I felt like a beautiful model on the runway with her king. My favorite pose was our foreheads pressed together. We stared dreamily into each other's eyes. Our smiles showed all the love we held in our hearts.

Our wedding ceremony and reception were held in a local vineyard. We went on a date to this vineyard for our six-month anniversary of dating. It was such a romantic location, with some of the most scenic views.

When Zach proposed to me on that special Tuesday morning , we knew at that moment where our wedding would be held. None of the other details mattered at that time, but they were worked out at a later date.

Laughter from the cocktail hour drifted over to where we were. The air-conditioned tent would be transformed from the ceremony area to the reception area in a matter of minutes while our guests enjoyed hors d'oeuvres and drinks. In just minutes, we'd be ready for all our guests to go back into the tent and wait for our grand entrance as husband and wife. What a grand entrance that would be.

Once everyone entered the tent, we walked over to the entrance.

The DJ quietened the room before an upbeat song came on.

"Introducing for the first time ever, Mr. and Mrs. Zachary Henry Miller."

We walked into the tent, holding hands. We raised our hands above our heads and did a small dance as we walked past our friends and family. Their faces glowed with love and excitement as they clapped and hollered out congratulations.

We made our way to the dance floor, where we went into our first dance. Zach had two left feet when it came to dancing. We had practiced our first dance hundreds of times to make sure it was perfect. Resting my head on Zach's chest, I relaxed. This was the perfect dance with the most perfectly imperfect man. We slow danced as the music serenaded our ears. Even though we were in a room full of people, it felt like we were the only individuals in the world.

I completed my father-daughter dance with both Robert and Dennis. Robert did the honors of walking me down the aisle, but I thought it was best for both to do the honors of dancing with me. Dennis hadn't been in my life for long, but he had been active these past two years.

After Zach danced with his mom, dinner was served plated style, and Zach's best man, Jake, gave a wonderful toast, and the party started.

We got up from our table, and we mingled with our guests.

"My only daughter is finally married," Mom gasped once she kissed my forehead. "She's married to a wonderful man, at that." Mom kissed Zach on the forehead.

Squeezing Zach's hand, I basked in the attention placed on us. It was our special day. The spotlight was on us tonight.

"I'm so glad to finally be a part of this family," Zach replied.

"Son, you were a part of this family when you saved our honey bun."

Robert's words. Was it his goal to make me cry more tears tonight? I had already cried more than enough.

"You have no idea how much that means to me."

Zach placed his hand over his heart.

Robert kissed my forehead before he hugged Zach. Robert was the father figure he had always desired, but never had. Hell, Robert was the best father figure in my life that I could've asked for. I wouldn't change anything about my childhood.

Dennis and Ashley stood. Ashley was tall compared to Dennis. She stood at least four inches taller than him.

"Congratulations, lovebug." Dennis hugged me.

"Welcome to the family," he said to Zach before he grabbed him into a hug.

"I'm glad to be a part of the family," Zach

responded.

Ashley called out her congratulations before she hugged us.

The relationship between Ashley and me was slowly progressing. It wasn't anything close to what Dennis and I had, but I was willing to accept and love anybody in Dennis' life.

We walked over to Eleanor and Benson. They both sipped on glasses of white wine.

Eleanor sat her wine down before she clasped her hands together.

"I'm forever grateful you came into my son's life," she whispered into my ear. "You taught him how to love again."

I beamed.

"He did the same for me," I admitted. "I was lost without him in my life."

She grabbed my hands and squeezed them.

"That is what it feels like when you haven't found your soulmate."

I glanced over Eleanor's shoulder at Benson. He laughed at something Zach had said.

"Do you think you've found the one?"

She smirked before she leaned in close.

"Sweetie, what I think and what I know are two different things. Only time will tell."

They had been dating for a year and a half. We had dinner with them a few times, and he seemed like a wonderful man. They were alike in some ways, but they were also different. She was more of an outgoing person, while he was laid back. One thing that they shared was their love of fitness. They were health nuts who met in the gym after seeing each other in passing for two months straight. They had been going to the same gym for four years. Once Benson's work schedule changed, they started going at the same time every day.

She kissed me on the cheek before she turned to Benson.

"Benson, give your congrats. They have other guests to mingle with."

Benson looked at me. He opened his muscular arms wide.

"Congratulations, Destiny." He pulled me into a bear hug, nearly suffocating me.

"Thank you," I choked out.

"Don't kill her, Benson." Eleanor swatted his arm. She grabbed her wine off the table. "Come on, I want you to meet someone."

Benson grabbed his wine before she grabbed his hand.

"Save me a dance," he called over his shoulder to me.

That I would do. The dance floor would be my friend tonight.

Zach wrapped his arm around my waist, grabbing my attention.

"Are you having a great time?"

I looked at him. Yesterday morning, he went to the barber and had his hair, beard, and mustache trimmed for the wedding. His long, brown hair was pulled back into a slick ponytail.

"I'm having the time of my life."

Zach cupped my chin and kissed me. His lips tasted just as amazing now as they did earlier.

"Would you consider this the best day ever?"

There were many days we experienced together that I could consider best.

"I'm not sure if today is the best day ever or the day you proposed."

Zach smiled. He tucked a curl behind my ear.

"That was a special day," he reminisced.

"It was the day you decided you wanted me to become your wife."

He settled his hands on my waist. He shook his head.

"No, it wasn't. I knew I wanted you to be my wife before I asked you on our first date."

He gave my waist a squeeze before he stepped closer.

"Seriously?"

"Yes. You would've thought I was completely out of my mind had I told you earlier."

I couldn't help but agree.

"Yeah."

He laughed before he kissed me on the neck.

"You weren't supposed to agree with me."

I laughed along with him.

"I couldn't help it."

Zach kissed my neck again. His lips brushed against the soft part of my neck, and my legs became weak.

"Zach…"

"What?"

"Lips off the beautiful bride," interrupted our

moment.

Jake, Emma, and Hannah stood behind us.

"I just can't help myself," Zach responded to Jake before they hugged.

Hannah blew me an air kiss before she grabbed me into a hug.

Emma smiled before she grabbed my hands.

"I'm sorry for the interruption. Jake couldn't be patient."

Jake agreed.

"Yeah. You two were taking too long to get to us."

We all laughed.

"My brother is finally hitched," Jake hollered before he patted Zach on the back.

"It took long enough," Zach agreed.

"The ceremony was so beautiful," Hannah gushed. "Come, dance with me."

Hanna and Emma pulled me onto the dance floor.

The night continued, and we were surrounded by our friends and family. I couldn't have asked for a better wedding.

Chapter Three

Destiny

"Here are your key cards."

The hotel attendant handed me two key cards. She clasped her hands together as she looked between Zach and me.

"I hope you have a wonderful honeymoon here at our hotel. We placed something special in your suite as a honeymoon gift. Enjoy your stay."

The bellhop grabbed our suitcases and placed them on a luggage cart and walked through the hotel lobby towards the elevators.

The hotel oozed with elegance. The hotel lobby's décor was modern, decorated with white and black furniture, paintings, and decorations. It wasn't a five-star hotel for no reason .

The elevator stopped on the fifteenth floor, and we walked to room 1512.

After inserting the key card, we gained access to our suite.

Walking into the massive suite, my breath was taken away. On the far side of the room was a king-sized bed decorated with red rose petals. A bathtub big enough to fit four people was located to the left of the bed. To the right was a kitchenette and a dining room table for two. On the table was an ice bucket holding a bottle of champagne. On the table were two flute glasses and a plate of chocolate-covered strawberries.

Seven months before our wedding, we searched long and hard for the best honeymoon destination for us. After three weeks of searching, we finally decided on Las Vegas, Nevada.

The bellhop pulled the luggage cart into the room. Zach handed him a tip, called out a thank you, and closed the door.

"This place is stunning," I commented as I placed my purse on the end table beside the front door.

It was everything I imagined for our honeymoon and more.

"Yes, it is," Zach agreed.

We walked further into the room. Zach

wrapped his arm around my waist and pulled me to his side. This would be our home for a week.

"I can't wait to try out this bed."

I smiled.

"We'll try it out later."

Zach nuzzled my neck, his mustache and beard tickling my sensitive spot.

"How about now?"

Before I could respond, Zach scooped me into his arms and laid me on the bed. The silky-smooth comforter and rose petals touched my skin. Zach hovered over me before he dipped his tongue into my mouth.

Zach had a touch of peppermint on his tongue from the mint he had just finished.

His tongue swirled into my mouth, sending me into a frenzy. I knew it would get hot and heavy during our honeymoon, but I never imagined it would be right after we walked into our suite.

"Zach." I gasped.

"Hm?"

He trailed kisses from my face to my neck, sending shivers up my spine. He wasn't the only one that desired contact, but we needed to start our honeymoon off right.

"Can we make a toast first?"

Zach groaned as he ducked his head. He growled against my ear.

"I'd rather have you first."

"Maybe after I devour one of those strawberries and have a sip of champagne."

Zach kissed my forehead before he got off me and helped me sit up.

We walked over to the table where Zach popped the cork. He poured champagne into our glasses, and we raised them up.

"Cheers to a life full of happiness. Through the good times and the bad, we'll never separate. We'll always be here for each other, through thick and thin."

Zach's toast was perfect. I couldn't have said it better myself.

"Cheers."

We clinked our glasses before we looped our arms and sipped our drink.

The bubbly goodness tasted amazing.

"Are you ready for a strawberry?" Zach asked.

"I was born ready."

Picking up a strawberry, we looped our arms again, and we fed each other.

We moaned in satisfaction as I stated, "That's a delicious strawberry."

I grabbed another one and popped it into my mouth.

Zach wrapped his arm around my waist, settling his hand on my hip.

"Can we get back to the bed now?" he whispered against my ear.

I swallow my strawberry.

"Didn't I say after my glass of champagne?"

"No, no." Zach shook his head. "I clearly remember you saying after you took a sip of your champagne."

This man and his attention to detail. That's the reason he was such an amazing detective for many years.

"I wasn't being literal."

I rubbed my nose against his. The move was subtle yet sweet. Rubbing my hand across his chin, I admired his handsome features. I fell in love with his soul. His looks were an added bonus.

"Everything that you say, I take literally."

I glanced over at the bed. It looked amazing, especially after the plane ride we endured. The plane ride was only an hour and a half long, but the process that it took to get onto the plane and fly tired me out.

I checked my watch. "We have reservations in thirty minutes."

Zach palmed my butt before he flicked his tongue against my ear.

"We can make it a quickie."

"Uh uh uh." I touched his nose with my index finger. "Our first time making love as husband and wife won't be a quickie."

I softly kissed his lips. He sucked in a sharp breath.

"I want it to be the best, sensual lovemaking we've ever done."

Zach smirked as he grabbed my chin and caressed it.

"Oh, that sounds tempting." Zach kissed me. "Tell me more."

My eyes flicked over to the bathtub.

"We can start in the bathtub. After a relaxing soak, make our way to that bed. We could do a nice massage before we get down to business."

Excitement danced in Zach's eyes. "It's official. You've convinced me to wait."

"Great. We have to get going now if we are going to make our reservation."

Grabbing Zach's hand, I pulled him towards the door.

"Why would you make us a reservation right after we checked into the hotel?"

Grabbing my purse, I squeezed his hand before I said, "If it were up to you, we wouldn't leave this room."

Zach laughed as we exited our room. "You got that right."

Taking the elevator down to the first floor, we walked out of the hotel and into the warm weather. The sun shined bright in the sky, bringing me excitement. Our kayak date would be nothing short of perfect. Shielding my eyes, I went into my purse and grabbed our sunglasses.

"Look at my wife, always prepared," he said as he put his sunglasses on.

We approached the valet and handed over our parking ticket.

"I just love hearing you call me your wife."

I'd never get tired of that title, no matter how many times he said it. That title meant the world to me now. Three years ago, I never imagined I'd be a wife. Hell, I couldn't see myself in a relationship. Now, I walked around with that title, and it felt amazing.

Zach slipped his arm around my waist. "You'll hear it every day from this point forward. I can assure you that."

Zach not only made me feel safe, but he also made me feel loved.

"You have no idea how much I look forward to that."

"You have so much more to look forward to," he said as the valet pulled our rental in front of the hotel.

"I do? Like what?"

Zach opened the passenger door, and he helped me inside the car.

"Oh, sweetheart, you'll see."

After Zach tipped the valet, he slipped into the driver's seat, and we headed for our destination.

***

My eyes widened as I looked down at the kayak in front of me.

The lake was calm, the complete opposite of how I felt inside. A bug buzzed in my ear, and I swatted at it.

Sweat gathered on my forehead. Wiping my now clammy hands on my jean shorts, I looked at Zach, his pearly white teeth showing.

"Uh..." I couldn't formulate one word. I wanted to be adventurous on this honeymoon. Staring down at the kayak, my spontaneous bone disappeared. What was I thinking?

"Are you chickening out on me?" Zach asked. He placed his hand on my lower back.

I motioned to the kayak.

"I didn't know this thing would be this small."

Zach laughed as he tightened my life vest. The vest was snug yet bearable. Hopefully, that's how it was supposed to be.

Zach rubbed his chin. "I'm sure you researched kayaks before you made the reservation."

I laughed.

"Yes, I did, but I don't recall them being this small."

"You'll be fine, I promise. I won't let anything happen to you."

He adjusted his life vest before sitting on the dock and lowered himself into the kayak. It shifted under his weight, quickening my heartbeat.

"On second thought…"

Looking around, I glanced at the trees that outlined the dock. Could I just grab onto one and hold on to it for dear life? Or until the kayak disappeared into thin air?

"Wife."

That one word. He had me smitten. I couldn't dare say no.

He held his hand out.

"Sit on the dock, and I'll help you in."

Trusting in Zach, I held my breath as I did as he instructed. With his assistance, I eased into the kayak and sat across from him.

"Are you okay?"

I looked out to the expansive lake. It looked relaxing, yet I'd rather explore the lake in a bigger form of transportation.

"Yes, I'm fine."

Zach's need for my reassurance never ceased to warm my heart.

Zach smiled. "Great."

He unhooked the kayak, and we slowly drifted away from the dock.

Zack handed me a paddle and showed me the ropes for moving through the water.

Within minutes, we paddled through the water in a rhythmic motion.

"This is actually relaxing," I commented.

The view of the lake was magical, thanks to the extensive, breathtaking mountains that shadowed the lively green trees.

If only I had brought my drawing supplies. This would be the perfect portrait to create and hang in our new home once we decide on one to buy.

We went to a showing days before the wedding. The three-bedroom, two-bath house oozed with so much potential, but there was too much work that needed to be done to meet the price the owners wanted. Buying a house was an important step in our marriage, and I wanted to ensure we would buy the perfect house for our future family.

"I'm glad you're enjoying it." Zach glanced towards the west. "I thought you were going to attach yourself to a tree and never let it go."

Matching my movements to Zach, I said, "I honestly considered it. How did you know?"

Zach smirked.

"I know everything about you."

I gave him a pointed look, waiting for more of an explanation.

"I saw the fear dance in your eyes. I couldn't help but take that fear away."

He took a deep breath as he stopped paddling. I followed suit.

"You have nothing to fear when you're with me. I'll protect you with my life."

No matter how many times he told me he would protect me with his life, it hit my heart the same way he had when he told me the first time we were at the police station.

"You've always protected me."

Looking into his eyes, sincerity and emotion danced in them. Some might say men don't have a sentimental and sensitive side, but Zach and I shared sentimental moments often. That's one of the reasons I loved him so much. He wasn't afraid to show me how much he cared.

"I promise I'll continue protecting you."

His protection began the night my best friend, Candace, was taken from me. It was an ordinary Tuesday night, and we decided to have dinner at our favorite sushi restaurant. After dinner, a masked gunman shot Candace and attempted to shoot me, but the gun jammed. After I made my escape on foot, I ended up at the police station, where Zach took me under his wing.

Even though encountering Zach turned out to be the best moment of my life, Candace passing away from her injuries turned out to be the worst moment of my life.

Thankfully, the assailant, who ended up being Zach's coworker's wife, Melissa, is now in prison. Zach's coworker, Trevor, tried to cover up his wife's actions since she went crazy over an affair that Trevor and Candace had. Melissa ended up with twenty years with the possibility of parole after those twenty years were completed for her part in Candace's death and Trevor ended up with ten years for attempting to cover up Melissa's crime.

"Destiny, come back to me, sweetheart."

Looking around, I saw a bald eagle swoop down from a tree and snatch up a small fish in its mouth.

Zach leaned forward and caressed my face.

"Were you thinking about Candace?"

I chuckled. He truly knew everything about me. I couldn't get anything past him.

"I was," I admitted, my chest feeling tight.

Zach touched my nose.

"Remember, do your breathing exercises."

I did as instructed, breathing in through my nose and out through my mouth with my eyes shut. My visits with my counselor over the past two years taught me so much.

Counseling after going back to Sacramento was necessary. At first, I didn't think I needed it. I thought I was strong enough to conquer my emotions with only Zach's help, but multiple nights of waking up with an irritated throat and tears streaming down my face proved me wrong.

After my first session with my counselor, we saw wonderful changes.

Opening my eyes, Zach stared at me.

"Are you feeling better?"

The tightness disappeared.

I nodded. "Thank you."

Zach leaned forward and kissed my forehead.

"Let's continue to explore."

Zach grabbed his paddle, and I followed suit.

"I can't wait for us to explore the wildlife."

That's exactly what we did over the next two hours.

Chapter Four

Zach

Coconut wafted into my nose as I stirred in bed. Humming, I ran my fingers through Destiny's curls.

Giving off a sleep-filled moan, Destiny turned around and pressed her butt against my growing erection.

After our kayaking date yesterday, we had just enough time to go to the hotel to clean up before we made our reservations at one of the best steakhouses in the area, according to our research.

Destiny wore a purple, A-line evening gown. With minimal makeup, she looked like a queen, with her hair pulled up into a twisted high bun. She wore my favorite pair of silver dangling earrings. I matched her with a purple short-sleeved dress shirt and black dress pants. To say we looked like a million bucks was an understatement.

We both ordered the steak, and after our dining experience, it was safe to say the food was exquisite, and the service was phenomenal.

Palming Destiny's butt, I kissed her exposed neck. I snaked my tongue out and licked her neck, and she stirred again.

My erection grew as her beautiful eyes, framed by her dark, thick lashes, fluttered open.

Stretching her arms above her head, her ample breasts rose as she yawned. Her hard nipples showed through the thin fabric of her lacy, pink negligee.

"What time is it?"

Her voice trembled with sleep.

Shrugging, I cupped her face and kissed her sweet, luscious lips.

"It's time for some lovemaking."

Her smile interrupted our kiss.

"Zach, no." She caressed my hand. Her eyes were hooded with love. "My breath. I haven't even brushed my teeth yet."

I kissed her again, savoring her taste. "Your

breath is fine."

I palmed her breasts before I flicked her nipple through her nightgown. She hissed as our gazes met.

"We have more important things to worry about."

Like your curvaceous hips, your delightful legs that make my knees buck, your gorgeous face that I can't seem to get enough of kissing.

Turning onto my back, I picked Destiny up with ease and placed her on top of me. She straddled me, looking at me as her hair fell over her shoulder.

Boy, I got to look and stare at this beauty for the rest of our lives. Damn, I was lucky.

She moved her hips in a seductive manner over my erection, sending me into a frenzy. I needed to be inside her.

"Like... This."

Leaning forward, I cupped her face, captured her mouth and pulled her down with me.

She panted as my tongue slipped into her mouth. I needed to take my time exploring her mouth and body, just like I did throughout the night and into the early morning.

Our mouths moved in sync, and I savored every bit of her mouth. I loved her taste, the way her breasts felt pressed against my chest, the way she ground on me.

The control I had to take it slow disappeared. We had our time last night after dinner to take things slow. We came back to the hotel room, soaked in a hot bath full of bubbles while we finished off our bottle of champagne and chocolate-covered strawberries. Once we made it over to the bed, we didn't get much sleep. We made love three times through the night, going into the morning. Now, it was time for round four.

Briefly pausing our kiss, I pulled Destiny's negligee over her head. Tossing the negligee to the ground, I stuffed my face into her breasts. I kissed them and flicked them with my tongue before I sucked one into my mouth. A loud moan escaped her mouth as she looked down at me.

"Oh gosh."

Her reactions only made my penis jerk more in my boxers.

"I need you," she said.

Lifting herself off my lap, Destiny pulled my boxers off in one swift motion. My erection sprang out, and Destiny didn't waste any time before she lowered herself on me.

I exhaled, her tight wetness sending me into a frenzy. No matter how many times we made love, every single time felt better than the last. Obsessed, that's how I felt.

Matching Destiny's rhythm, her moans filled the room. Her breasts bounced up and down as I plummeted into her. Everything about her was perfect, from the way she formed an O with her mouth when pleasure tingled within her to how she held onto my hands tight for balance.

"I'm about to…"

Destiny screamed before she lost all control

of her body. Releasing my hands, she fell onto my chest.

Euphoria washed over me as I lost all control. Running my fingers through Destiny's hair, I kissed her nose before I wrapped my arms around her and held her tight.

***

Hot water washed over my body as I closed my eyes. Running my fingers through my hair, I washed out the last of the conditioner.

Peeking an eye open, Destiny stood in front of me under her own stream of water. Her nipples stood alert as she ran her fingers through her own hair.

Leaning forward, I planted a feather-soft kiss on Destiny's lips and smiled. She opened her eyes, and a smirk touched her lips.

Our hotel room wasn't only equipped with a huge bathtub, but we also had dual shower heads in the shower.

"I think I want to have a shower like this in our new house," she commented.

There wasn't any reason for us to do the installation in our current home since we planned to put it on the market as soon as we found the perfect home for us.

"I'll make anything happen for you, sweetheart."

"Thank you."

Destiny turned her back to me. My eyes danced up her luscious body, from her feet to the top of her head. Snaking my arm around her waist, I pressed myself up against her. Our bodies fit perfectly, like puzzle pieces.

"What are you doing?" she asked.

She looked over her shoulder and rubbed my forearms. She snaked her tongue out and licked my lips.

"I'm just giving my wife some attention."

She giggled, no doubt loving my reference to her being my wife.

"You've given me enough attention for the past..." she stated, then was silent for a few seconds. "Twelve hours."

Kissing Destiny's cheek, I rubbed her hip. I loved everything about her, from her cute laugh to the endless love she gave.

"When have you ever complained about too much attention?"

Destiny shut the water off before she turned around and looked at me.

"When we have a few hours to get ready, eat a late breakfast, and get to our reservation."

We stepped out of the shower, and I handed Destiny her towel. The towel resembled something extremely soft, like a fluffy kitten. It wasn't your average towel that you'd stumble upon while strolling through a department store.

"You have a point," I agreed.

"What are we doing today?"

Destiny wrapped her towel around her body and opened the bathroom door. Immediately, cold air drifted into the bathroom.

"Uh uh."

Turning around, she looked at me.

I shook my head.

"You don't get to find out what we're doing until we're en route."

"Are you afraid I'm going to chicken out?"

She wiggled her eyes before she stuck her tongue out at me.

"Maybe." I winked at her. "Maybe not."

"Can I get a hint?"

I wrapped my towel around my waist. "No hints. Even though you didn't hold up your end of the bargain, it doesn't mean I'm not going to hold up mine."

Several weeks before the wedding, we decided that we would each plan out specific days. Yesterday, Destiny had planned out our kayak trip, followed by our steakhouse dinner. Today, I had a helicopter tour planned for us. Destiny had never been on a helicopter. When we went back to Sacramento and moved in together, she told me she had traveled by plane quite a few times to visit her parents, but she had never been on a helicopter. Today, that would change. She just didn't know it yet.

"Ugh, fine." She poked out her lip. "I guess I have to wait to find out."

"Only for another two hours."

Destiny and I dried and did our hair for the day before we dressed in matching colors. I wore a navy blue t-shirt with black khaki shorts, and she wore a navy blue short romper that made every curve on her body stand out.

Walking hand in hand, we made our way downstairs to the breakfast café.

Once we were led to our table by the hostess, I pulled out the chair for Destiny.

She winked at me as she said, "Thank you, sweetie."

"Anything for you."

After our waitress brought out our coffee, Destiny ordered an oatmeal with a fruit parfait on the side. I ordered a hearty plate of bacon, eggs, potatoes and toast.

Destiny planted her beautiful eyes on me.

"What's going through your mind?"

Taking a sip of my coffee, I winced. It was hot and strong, exactly how I desired it.

Destiny tapped her fingers on the table.

"I'm trying to figure out what we're doing today."

I laughed. "You're not going to figure it out. You'll never guess what we're doing."

Destiny raised her eyebrow as she added sugar to her coffee.

"Are you sure about that?"

Winking at her, I replied, "Of course, I'm sure."

Destiny stirred her coffee before she took a sip. "Am I allowed to guess?"

"Be my guest. I'm ready to hear all your thoughts."

Destiny smiled before she sipped her coffee and placed it on the table.

"Are we going rock climbing?"

I shook my head. "That is a great suggestion, but no."

"Am I somewhat close? On the spontaneous aspect?"

I sipped my coffee. "I'm not giving you any hints."

Destiny scoffed. She twirled a loose curl around her index finger. Today, she wore her hair in a high ponytail with ringlets hanging in her face. This hairstyle was one of my favorites on her.

She tapped her cheek, deep in thought.

"Are we going skydiving?"

"No." I sipped my coffee. "You'll find out in about an hour."

Our food arrived shortly after. While we ate, Destiny suggested more date ideas. She suggested a movie date to gambling at the casino.

"Why would I plan a movie date when we can go back home to do that?"

Destiny laughed, her laugh was infectious. I couldn't wait to hear that laugh for the rest of my life. It had warmed my insides for the past two years.

"I don't know." She ate a piece of fruit. "I'm pulling at straws right now."

I ate a piece of bacon. "You'll find out soon."

After we finished eating, we paid for our food and exited the cafe.

Once valet brought our car, I programmed our location into the GPS system.

Destiny squealed as she clapped her hands.

She wiggled with excitement in the passenger seat.

"Oh my gosh. Are we really going on a helicopter tour?"

I couldn't help but smile at her excitement. This is what I lived for every day. I lived to make Destiny happy.

"I've never been on a helicopter before," she gasped.

I pulled out of the hotel parking lot, heading in the direction of our destination.

"I know. That's why I'm making it happen today."

Destiny placed her hand on my knee and squeezed it.

"You're the best."

Glancing over at Destiny, I winked before I focused on the road.

"That's all you."

We drove to our destination, listening to country music. Once we arrived, Destiny's eyes widened.

As I pulled into the parking lot, I observed the helicopter sitting on top of the two-story building.

After I stepped out of the car, I opened Destiny's door.

Placing her hand in mine, she stepped out of the car.

"I can't believe this is happening."

Squeezing Destiny's hand, I kissed her cheek.

"It's happening, sweetheart."

After we walked into the building, we were greeted by an attendant. Once we signed the waivers, we were escorted upstairs.

I swung the door open, and Destiny's eyes widened. She brought her hands up to her mouth in awe. A pilot stood beside the helicopter, holding two glasses of red wine.

Once we approached, he handed us the glasses.

"Are you two newlyweds ready for the helicopter tour?" he asked.

Destiny took a sip of her wine.

"I was born ready."

Wrapping my arm around her waist, I said, "Yes, let's get this party started."

Our pilot helped Destiny climb in before I hopped in behind her. A charcuterie board of meats, cheese, and crackers sat in front of us.

"Shall we propose a toast?" I asked. Raising my glass, Destiny followed suit.

"We shall."

"Let's toast to this wonderful helicopter tour that I get to take with my beautiful wife."

Destiny leaned forward and rubbed her nose against mine. She kissed me softly.

"Cheers."

We clinked our glasses and took a sip.

Over the next hour, our pilot flew us over Lake Mead, Hoover Dam, and the Las Vegas Strip.

The view was beautiful, nothing like I had ever imagined. The last time I had been in a helicopter, it was work related. We were searching for a suspect. I couldn't believe I sat with my arm wrapped around my wife. This feeling was indescribable. This was only the start of the rest of our lives. I couldn't wait to see what the future held for us.

Chapter Five

Destiny

"How does it feel being back from your honeymoon?" Emma asked.

Emma, Hannah, and I hung out at Emma's house. It was Friday night, and we were having our monthly girl's night. Aiden and Jayden were at Emma's parents' house for the night, so we had the entire house to ourselves. We hung out in the living room, playing catch up.

Grabbing my glass of ice water, I took a sip.

"It's bittersweet," I admitted. "The honeymoon was magnificent. We had so much fun, but it was time to get back to our normal day-to-day routine."

We had a blast during our honeymoon. We visited several museums in the area, admiring the paintings, sculptures, and history that they held. Zach ended up winning a thousand dollars on our second-to-last night in town after we hit up five casinos. We dined at amazing restaurants, ranging from Italian cuisine to Korean cuisine. After stepping out of my comfort zone, Greek cuisine was now a new favorite of mine. On our last night, we enjoyed a couple's massage at the spa. While our masseuses massaged all the stress out of our muscles, we listened to a relaxing tempo.

"I'm glad you had a wonderful time," Hannah said.

Hannah sat in the Lazy Boy chair on the other side of the coffee table. Emma and I sat on the loveseat.

Our monthly nights were usually spent out in the town, dining at a new restaurant we wanted to try or participating in a new activity. Tonight, we were at Emma's house. We had the place to ourselves since Zach and Jake were out doing their own thing.

Zach and I came back to town late Saturday night. We slept away most of our Sunday morning. Bright and early on Monday morning, we watched the sunrise. Going into the evening, we walked the sunset. On Tuesday morning, we were back at work. Our honeymoon lasted a week. It was one of the best weeks of my life, but I had to get back to work. I missed my students.

"What were you two up to when I was out of town?"

I placed my glass on the coffee table and sat crisscross applesauce on the couch. I considered Emma's house and Hannah's apartment my second home, so being comfortable was my forte.

The aroma of chicken swirled in the living room, a quick reminder that dinner would be ready shortly.

"Chasing after my twin boys," Emma commented. "They were invited to a birthday party, and all the children went wild."

"Where was the birthday party?" I asked.

"At the zoo."

Hannah gasped as she placed her right leg over her left leg. "I wish I'd had a birthday party at the zoo when I was younger," she commented.

"Yeah, right?" I agreed. "I was thrown birthday parties at parks."

"It was the boy's second time visiting the zoo. They went a few years back, but they had the time of their life." Emma shrugged. "I actually enjoyed the zoo as well."

"What's been occupying you?" I asked Hannah.

Hannah smirked, immediately giving me the answer without even opening her mouth and voicing it. She looked off to the side before she brought her hand up to her mouth to hide her growing smile.

"Dating my ass off," Hannah finally answered.

Emma scoffed before she motioned to Hannah. "Stand up."

Hannah gave a confused look before she dragged her fingers through her blonde hair and stood.

"Turn to the side."

Hannah did as Emma said, and she struck a pose.

"Your ass is still there."

We all laughed as Hannah sat down.

"How many dates did you go on?" I asked.

Hannah silently counted on her fingers. When she moved from one hand with all her fingers out to the other, Emma and I tried our hardest to hold in our laughter.

"Only two."

Emma and I exchanged a look. The laughter that I tried my hardest to hold inside erupted.

"What?" Hannah asked, laughing herself.

"Nothing, nothing."

Hannah's dramatics were the reasons I loved our friendship so much.

"How did those two dates go?" Emma asked after she took a sip of her wine.

Tonight, Emma and Hannah sipped wine. I sipped on water, recovering from all the alcohol I drank last week.

Right before Hannah could answer, the oven

beeped.

"Dinner's ready," Hannah said as she rose from her seat.

Grabbing our drinks, we walked into the kitchen. The kitchen was huge, composed of stainless-steel appliances and modern cabinets.

Tonight, we had chicken Caesar salad with bread.

Emma pulled the chicken breast out of the oven. While Emma sliced the chicken, Hannah sliced the bread, and I made the salad. Together, we made the perfect team.

Within minutes, we sat at the dinner table with plates of delicious food in front of us.

"So, how did the dates go?" I asked as I cut into my chicken.

"The first one was..." Hannah shrugged. "Meh. The second one was better than I expected."

She forked salad into her mouth.

"That's progress," Emma stated as she smiled.

"When is the next date?" I asked as I ate a piece of chicken.

Hannah gave me a pointed look. "Who says there will be a second date?"

"Your rosy cheeks," I pointed out.

Hannah attempted to cover her smile, but it was no use.

"Tell us all about him," Emma said as she took a bite of her bread.

"Right now, I want to keep some details a

secret. At least for a little while. I want to make sure this is something I'm interested in before I tell you two about him."

"There's nothing wrong with that," I replied as I took another bite of my food. "Just make sure you're taking the necessary precautions."

Hannah placed her hand on mine and gave me a sympathetic smile.

"I promise I will."

Precautions from me were handed out often. My best friend Candace didn't take the precautions handed to her by others. For some reason, she never thought harm would come her way. Sadly, she learned the hard way, and she was no longer alive. For this, I offered precautions every chance I got. I didn't want another senseless crime to happen to my friends or anyone else if I could help it.

"Just know, I'm dating with intent."

"Are you sure about that?" Emma pointed her fork at Hannah. "You've gone on more dates than Destiny and I combined."

Hannah couldn't help but laugh. "I know that's true, but I have to find Mr. Right. He's not easy to find nowadays."

"You're right about that," I admitted before I sipped my water.

Falling in love with Zach wasn't anticipated. It happened when I least expected it, but the love hit me hard. Zach came into my life when I needed him the most. I could never thank him enough for that.

"How did you know Jake was the one?" Hannah asked Emma.

Emma finished chewing her food before she responded.

"I saw him across the courtyard during the first week of my last year of college. I thought, what a handsome guy, but I was never one to approach a guy. Not even a week later, we ran into each other while headed to class. The books we carried fell out of our hands and he picked them up."

"What happened next?" I asked.

I was invested in their love story. I'd seen many movies about how couples fell in love over the years, but I knew it was all fictional. Their love story wasn't.

"The books we dropped were identical." Emma took a sip of her wine. "We took the same class but at different times. Somehow, he handed me his book, and he took my book."

"How did you get your book back?" Hannah asked before she took a bite of her bread.

"Jake hunted me down," she said with a wink. "He found me one morning when I walked to my first class of the day. He gave me my book back. I hadn't realized the book I had wasn't my book, so I was surprised when he approached me. We chatted for all of two minutes before he asked me for my number. The rest is history."

"Oh my gosh." I placed my hand over my heart. "That's the cutest story I've ever heard," I admitted.

"Seriously," Hannah agreed. "Ugh, I'm totally jealous. How did you two find your prince charming and I'm over here fantasizing about it? I'm trying to find my prince charming too, damn it."

"You never know. It might be the guy that gave you the better-than-expected date," I pointed out.

Hannah smiled.

"Maybe."

Silence settled for a moment before Hannah asked another question. Her eyes bounced back and forth between Emma and me.

"How did you two know you were in love?"

I've never been asked that question before. Possibly because I'd never felt anything remotely similar to love until Zach came into my life.

"I knew I was in love when I realized I couldn't go another day without Jake being in my life."

Hannah looked at me, waiting for my response.

"I was never one to settle down in a relationship," I began. "Nobody had ever caught my attention like Zach had. When I was around him, I felt feelings for him I never felt for anyone else. My heart yearned for him. That's when I knew I was in love."

Hannah grasped our hands and squeezed them. "You two give me so much hope."

We continued to talk while we ate dinner. After dinner, we walked back into the living room and hung out. It was nothing better than getting together with the ladies and just having fun.

It took me some time to warm up to the idea of getting together with Hannah and Emma. When I first met Emma, I knew we'd get along, no problem. Our men weren't best friends for nothing. By default, I knew we'd learn to love each other for the sake of our men. We quickly learned that we had more than our men's friendship in common.

Hannah and Emma met five years ago. They met while they attended a yoga class together. For one of the exercises, they had to work in pairs. Hannah and Emma gravitated towards each other and bonded while performing the double tree pose. They've been inseparable ever since.

Their friendship reminded me a lot of the friendship Candace and I shared. Boy, I missed Candace so much. She's been gone more than two years now. Not a day went by without me thinking about her.

At first, I felt guilty for having fun. How was I supposed to have fun when my best friend could no longer experience it? How was I supposed to walk around with a smile on my face when my best friend could no longer smile or experience any feelings?

How did my best friend die from a horrendous crime? How did I escape? Some might say it wasn't my time, but I couldn't fathom how it could've been Candace's time. She was too young and had many things going for her.

The only two people I could talk about my feelings with concerning Candace were Zach and my counselor.

Zach being my other half, he could easily sense when something was off with me. It didn't feel right to talk to Hannah or Emma about how I felt. Yes, they told me that I could talk to them about anything. That was one of the amazing reasons for having friends, being able to talk and vent to them if need be. Candace was just a topic that I chose to keep between Zach and my counselor.

I could never thank my counselor enough for all that she had done for me. I still saw her occasionally and the guidance she had provided had helped me gain strategies to deal with the trauma I suffered with to this day.

All in all, with the help of my friends and family, I knew I would be fine. Their love was everything I needed.

Chapter Six

Zach

"Hole-in-one," Jake called out.

He raised his arms in the air and cheered while he held tight onto his cue stick.

Jake and I were having a guy's night out. Destiny, Emma and Hannah were at Jake's house having their own get-together. The twins were at Jake's in-law's house for the night. Jake and I decided we would love to play some pool, so we headed to a local bar in town. For a Friday night, the place wasn't nearly as packed as I had expected. Maybe it had to do with multiple bars occupying this town.

"Hole-in-one is a golf term," I pointed out as I leaned my cue stick on the pool table.

"Yeah…" Jake thought for a moment. "I still won, though."

Laughing, I grabbed my beer and took a swig. "I think someone might've already had one too many already."

We were there an hour. Jake was on his fourth beer, and I was still on my first.

Jake shrugged before he grabbed his beer. "Great thing you're driving tonight. I'm allowed to drink as much as I like."

"As long as I don't have to clean puke out of my truck or carry you into your house, you're good."

Jake patted me on the back.

"I'm a pro now. You don't have to worry about that."

He placed his cue stick on the pool table and walked over to our table.

"You haven't always been able to handle your alcohol."

I sat across from him and finished off the last of my beer.

"What time are you referring to?" he asked.

There were several times that I could think of, from our high school days when we shouldn't have been drinking at those lake parties to months before the twins were born.

"When you found out you were having two babies instead of one."

Jake laughed. "You're right about that time. I thought I would pass out after learning about the twins."

When Jake found out they were having twins at the gender reveal party they hosted, he got wasted. He was prepared to have one child, but he didn't know what he'd do with two babies at the same age, at the same time. It's safe to say he's learned how to take care of twins. He's such a great father. One day, if Destiny and I decided to have a baby, I knew who to come to about parenting. I didn't have my own father in my life to learn from, but Jake learned from his father.

"Or when you got so wasted at the end of the school year bash."

Jake motioned his hands in the air, signaling for our waitress to come to our table.

"Tye always threw the best parties. We had to celebrate graduating high school. We deserved that party. Our senior year was hell."

Our waitress walked over to the table. She set a plate of hot wings in front of us before Jake ordered us both another beer before our waitress walked away.

The hot sauce scent burned my nose, and I winced. I couldn't wait to devour them.

"It wasn't all bad," I pointed out as I grabbed a wing and took a bite. "We did grad bash like two weeks before graduation."

Jake grabbed a wing. "Yeah. One great event

out of all the torture we had to endure."

Raising an eyebrow, I asked, "Would it be appropriate to consider the hard work we did torture?"

"Yeah, considering I nearly pulled out all my hair when we had to take our end-of-year exams, the SATS, ACTs."

I pointed at the top of his head. "Is that why you're starting to bald on the top of your head?"

Jake laughed as he rubbed his hand over his temple-faded hairstyle.

"You're an asshole. I'm not balding."

I finished off my wing and went for another.

"Yet." I winked at him. "You forgot to add yet."

Jake grabbed a bottle top off the table and tossed it across the table at me.

"Everyone wasn't blessed with long silky hair like yourself."

Our waitress dropped off our two beers. Jake grabbed his beer and immediately opened it up.

"Miss, before you go," I said, stopping our waitress in her tracks. "Can we have two glasses of water?"

She nodded. "Yes, I'll be right back."

"What's with the waters?" Jake asked before he took a sip of his beer.

A loud whoop echoed throughout the bar, temporarily distracting me.

"You need to stay hydrated with all the alcohol you're drinking."

"What are you turning into, a grandpa?" he asked.

Shaking my head, I laughed. "No, I'm just trying to make sure your hangover that you'll have tomorrow is as mild as possible."

"Back to my long, silky-smooth hair. It took me a long time to grow it this long," I pointed out as I opened my beer.

This was my last beer of the night, and I needed to nurse it. Two beers were always my limit when I was the designated driver. The next time we went out, Jake would be the designated driver. We always took turns.

"What has it been, more than fifteen years?"

"Yes." I thought for a moment. "Damn, we're getting old."

"Hey, speak for yourself, buddy. I feel the same now as I did when I was twenty-one."

By the time I devoured my second wing, the waitress brought our waters to the table.

"Drink."

Jake playfully rolled his eyes before he sat his beer on the table and gulped down some water.

"You need to drink too, old man," he joked.

"Ha ha ha." I grabbed my water and sipped some of it.

"So, how was the honeymoon?" Jake asked.

This was the first time we'd gotten together since Destiny and I arrived back from our honeymoon. The day that we flew back to town, we arrived late. So, we slept away most of the following day. Monday morning, we were able to watch the sunrise. On Tuesday, I went back to the police station, and Destiny went back to school.

"It was perfect."

The honeymoon exceeded my expectations, and I couldn't wait for the next trip where we'd take some time off from work and have fun.

"Perfect? Wow. That's amazing." Jake smiled.

"It was everything we imagined and more."

"Did you two hit up any of the casino's out there?" Jake asked as he grabbed another wing.

"Yes, we went to five." I took a swig from my beer.

"Did you win anything worth celebrating?"

I shrugged. "A thousand dollars."

Jake widened his eyes. "You're saying a thousand dollars nonchalantly like it's nothing."

A group of rowdy young men walked through the door. They made a beeline across the bar to a table tucked off in the corner. It was evident they were regulars.

"It's something, but I hoped for the big payout."

Jake devoured his wing, leaving a trail of buffalo sauce on his cheek.

"One day, Zach. It'll happen one day."

I motioned to his cheek. "You have a little something on your face."

Jake snorted. "Thanks." He grabbed a napkin and wiped his face. "Did you two do anything spectacular? Out of the ordinary?"

"I took her on a helicopter ride."

"Seriously?"

Jake smiled.

"Yes." I sat back, getting comfortable in my seat. "It was her first time being in a helicopter. We enjoyed the tour while we drank wine and ate some appetizers."

"I'll be damned. My boy knows how to romance his wife."

"I would say I learned from my best friend but…"

Jake and I laughed.

"Hell, you better say you learned from me." He took a sip of his beer. "All the time you'd be at the house with Emma and the kids. I knew, eventually, something I did would rub off on you."

I smiled. "All it took was the most amazing woman to grace me with her presence."

Destiny and my life changed on a fateful Tuesday night, days after Christmas. Trevor, my old partner at the time, walked into my office and informed me that a frazzled woman ran into the police station in need of my assistance. When I laid eyes on her, my heart dropped into my chest. Never had I ever seen such a beautiful woman in my life. I knew I was fascinated with her. I refused to let her out of my sight.

"Earth to Zach. Stop daydreaming. You're practically drooling over there."

"Shut up, I'm not drooling…" I wiped at my mouth, not sure if Jake was kidding or serious.

"What were you daydreaming about?" he asked.

Taking a sip of my beer, I folded my hands

on the table. "The first time Destiny and I met," I admitted.

Jake and I joked around with each other a lot, but our friendship was built on more than just laughter. There were times when we laughed until our stomach ached and there were times when we cried our hearts out. Through it all, our friendship never wavered. I couldn't ask for a better friend.

Jake grabbed another wing. "In reality, that was a horrible time, especially for Destiny, but if the situation hadn't occurred, I doubt you two would have ever met."

Jake was right. During the time that Destiny lost her best friend, I came into her life. She needed protection. I refused to allow anyone else to do the protecting. She needed the best protection that could be provided. Only I could provide that protection. If I had allowed the only officer in the department to take her into protective custody, things wouldn't have turned out positive for Destiny. The person who ended up killing Destiny's best friend, Candace, was the police officer's wife. Candace and Trevor were in an illicit relationship. Trevor's wife, Melissa, didn't take too kindly to this relationship and decided to take matters into her own hands when she realized their relationship wasn't coming to an end anytime soon.

It wasn't often, but sometimes, I wondered if she ever sat down and thought about the reason we met. Even though she said yes when I asked for her hand in marriage, I hoped she'd never regret her decision.

"Yeah, we probably wouldn't have."

With Destiny being a teacher and my previously being a lead detective, we wouldn't have had a reason for our paths to cross. Destiny wasn't involved in any criminal activities, so she never had to come to the police station. I didn't have any children for us to meet at her job. She wasn't the type to hang around bars 24/7. From what I knew, she occasionally went to hang out with Candace on the nights she worked as a bartender. She hadn't stepped into a bar since. I only went out to the bar to hang out with Jake.

I wouldn't have approached her if I had gone to a bar and spotted Destiny. There were some women that I laid eyes on, and I could easily tell that their intent for the night was to have a one-night stand. Destiny didn't give off that type of energy.

With my lack of desire to find love, I wouldn't have even wasted Destiny's time. It was crazy to find out Destiny wasn't into relationships as well. Our lack of desire to find love resulted from us struggling with trust, but for different reasons. Destiny's trust issues resulted from her father leaving her at a young age because he wasn't ready to step up and take on that father figure role. He has since redeemed himself in the past two and a half years. My lack of trust came from my ex-girlfriend, but Destiny worked magic on me and made me a new man.

After finishing off our plate of wings and drinks, we headed out of the bar. Jake walked with a little hobble, the alcohol he consumed catching up to him.

"Are you sure you'll not get sick in my truck?" I asked him.

He laughed. "I'm sure."

Once we made it to my truck, Jake opened the passenger door. He pulled himself into the cab before giving me a thumbs-up and slammed the door.

The trip to Jake's house was eventful. During the entire drive, he talked about the horrible customers he received at the phone store he managed over the past few days.

"You seriously wouldn't believe how crazy people go over their phones," Jake said as we pulled into the driveway.

Oddly, it was only Emma's car in the driveway. It was unusual for Destiny to leave a location without letting me know, but sometimes she did forget.

That only meant Destiny was most likely at home, waiting for me to arrive. Hopefully, she'd be in a thin piece of lingerie that I could break with my teeth… or in nothing at all.

Nothing at all sounded better.

"Do you need me to help you walk to the front door?"

Jake opened the passenger door and turned to look at me. "No, I'm fine. I can manage."

"Go ahead and sleep it off. Call me tomorrow

when your hangover goes away."

"I will."

Jake hobbled to the front door. When he managed to put his key into the door after the fourth try, I left Jake's house.

I drummed my fingers on the steering wheel as I drove, along to the beat of the music that played as I drove home.

Passing by the house on the street, I noticed no lights were on in the house, but Destiny's car sat in its usual space in the driveway. Why was Destiny in the house with no lights on? Maybe she wanted to surprise me. I parked beside Destiny's car and killed the ignition.

As I walked along the sidewalk, my heart dropped into the pit of my stomach. The hair on my arms rose as I squatted down and analyzed the contents scattered in the front yard. My mouth went dry as I stared at Destiny's purse and discarded car keys.

Pulling my phone away from my mouth as I stood up, I called the number I knew by heart.

"Hello, Frank." I exhaled. "I need you to come to my house. Bring backup."

"What's going on?"

"I think someone has kidnapped Destiny."

Chapter Seven

Zach

Crime scene tape outlined our entire front yard. Red and blue lights lit up the entire street like Christmas lights. Police cars littered the front of our street and the driveway. Neighbors from the surrounding houses stood on the road, looking at the scene with curiosity and fear in their eyes.

"Do you really think we'll be able to get fingerprints off her purse and keys?" I asked Frank.

So much was going on so fast that I didn't know what to do with myself. I was losing my mind.

"There is a slight chance that if Destiny was attacked, the person could've placed her items just like this as a rogue to distract us."

If? There's no way that Frank just said if. His choice of words had to have been a mistake. This wasn't like Destiny just to up and disappear, especially in this manner. Especially after everything she's gone through. There was no if about it. Destiny was attacked. The question was, where was my wife?

Frank slipped on a pair of gloves before he picked up Destiny's keys and examined them. Her favorite keychain accessory, a flower, glinted in the red and blue lights.

He held his hand out to the police officer who stood with us and handed him an evidence bag. He slipped Destiny's key into the bag before he handed it back to the police officer.

"I don't have a great feeling about this," I commented. "Something's not right."

Darting my eyes around the yard, eyes bore into my soul. The elderly couple two doors down stood in their robes, holding hands. This didn't feel right.

Frank picked up Destiny's purse. He turned it around and there was a grass stain on its side.

"There was a scuffle," I observed.

Cursing under my breath, I stalked away from Frank, fuming. I prayed to the heavens above that

Destiny was okay. She had to be okay. She was my everything, and nothing could happen to her. If anything happened to her…

"That might be the case," Frank interrupted my thoughts.

Frank opened the purse and rummaged through it. He pulled out Destiny's phone. He turned it from the back to the front, examining it. When I noticed the screen was shattered, I reached out to grab the phone, but Frank pulled the phone out of my reach.

"This is evidence."

"Someone attacked my freaking wife," I seethed.

Balling up my fist, my blood boiled. All I could see was red. "Evidence doesn't mean shit to me right now."

"We must follow proper protocol. Get the evidence…"

Frank's lips continued to move, but I didn't hear anything that came out of his mouth.

Proper protocol was followed when my loved ones weren't in danger. My wife was in danger. Her phone was cracked, so there had to have been a struggle. The last thing I cared about was proper protocol. I needed to find her fast. Proper protocol didn't mean anything to me.

Frank placed Destiny's phone and purse in separate evidence bags.

"We should have some information in…"

I walked away from Frank, feeling completely disrespected. Calling Frank or anyone else in the department to assist with locating Destiny was a waste of time. I couldn't wait weeks for information to come out about my wife. I needed the information tonight. There was no way possible I could go to sleep without knowing Destiny was okay.

How did I know if she was okay? How did I know she wasn't in harm's way? Or worse, how did I know she wasn't dead?

There wasn't any blood that was found, but that didn't mean anything. The person responsible could've kidnapped Destiny and taken her somewhere to…

I had to do my own searching. Protocol wasn't something I could follow, no matter what.

Even though I was no longer a lead detective, it didn't mean I couldn't get down and dirty with my wife's case. My expertise hadn't gone away since I became an assistant chief. In all honesty, I loved being a lead detective, but I respected Destiny's fear too much. It was time to come out of retirement.

First things first, I needed to contact Emma and Hannah. They were the last ones, to my knowledge, who saw Destiny.

Emma's phone rang twice before she answered.

"If you're calling to check up on Jake, he just puked for the second time." She paused for a brief second before chuckling. "Now he's passed out in the bathtub. What did you do to my husband?"

I'd love to joke with her if the situation wasn't serious. Jake's tolerance for alcohol wasn't as great as he thought it was. With age came changes.

"I need to talk to you about Destiny."

I needed to address the issue at hand.

"Is something wrong?" Her voice was laced with worry.

Swallowing the huge lump in my throat, I responded, "Destiny's missing."

The silence was deadly.

"What do you mean missing? What happened?"

"That's why I'm calling you. I'm not sure what happened. After I dropped Jake off, I came home and found her belongings scattered on the sidewalk in front of the house. I've called for backup, and we can't find her."

"Oh my gosh. Was she kidnapped? Was she…"

I interrupted her spew of words. Emma could talk a mile a minute when overwhelmed, but we didn't have time for that. Time was ticking. Quicker than I'd prefer.

"She didn't text me on her way home like she usually does. Did anything seem off with her before she left?"

"No, everything was normal. We had a wonderful girl's night. She didn't mention anything was bothering her or that something was awry."

Cursing under my breath, I turned and looked over my shoulder. Frank talked to two police officers. He moved his hands animatedly while he spoke. The police officers listened before they nodded their heads and walked away from him.

"Do you recall what time she left the house?"

Time was key in cases as such. If we could narrow down a specific timeframe for the events that occurred, we might be able to use those times to our advantage.

"Hannah and Destiny left..." she paused. "A little after eight, I believe."

"Give me a second."

Going to my call log, I clicked on my call to Frank's phone. I called him at 8:47PM. The trip from Jake's house to our house is a fifteen-minute drive.

Approximately twenty-five minutes were unaccounted for between Destiny's estimated arrival and my arrival.

Did Destiny immediately get out of the car when she first arrived home? Did she sit in the car for a few minutes, doing something on her phone?

So many questions, yet I had no answers. I needed answers.

"Did you hear from Destiny after she left your house?"

"No, she didn't reach out to me."

I had an estimated timeframe from Emma. Now, it was time to call Hannah.

"Thank you for taking my call, Emma. I'm going to call Hannah now."

"Please, keep me updated, Zach."

Emma's voice cracked on my name, a telltale sign she was on the verge of tears.

"I will, I promise."

After I dialed Hannah's number, I closed my eyes, willing the horrific thoughts that crowded my head to dissipate. Destiny could be anywhere by now. I had no idea what environment she was in. If she was still all—

"Hello Zach, what's up."

Hannah's voice was cheerful, the opposite of how I felt inside.

"Destiny's missing."

"What?" Hannah yelled into my phone, forcing me to pull the phone away from my ear from her pitch.

"Her purse and car keys were scattered on the front lawn when I arrived. I don't know where she is. I can't find her."

"How the hell did this happen? I just saw her not even an hour ago."

More questions were being asked, yet no answers could be provided.

"Did Destiny say anything to you out of the ordinary?"

"No, she didn't say anything to me."

"Thank you, I have to go."

I hung up after Hannah asked me to keep her updated and call her whenever I needed.

The last two people I knew who saw Destiny couldn't tell me anything. From their recollection, everything seemed normal. How could everything seem normal less than an hour ago? My life had changed for the worse. My other half was missing in action, and I had no idea where she was.

Frank motioned for me to approach him. Reluctantly, I placed one foot in front of the other and walked over to him.

"I'll need to ask you some questions about your wife."

Usually, I was the one who asked the questions. Now, I was being questioned. How could I be questioned about my wife's disappearance? This was unreal.

Was I dreaming? Was I stuck in a horrible nightmare, waiting to wake up? Pinching myself, pain resonated. This was a nightmare I couldn't force myself to wake up from. I was living it.

"Shall we go inside and sit down?"

Frank looked around the yard at all the curious eyes. Everyone within a three-house radius on both sides of our house and across the street was outside, being onlookers.

"We shall."

Before we went into the house, Frank tasked some of the police officers to ask the neighbors if they had seen anything.

Unlocking the house, we walked to the dining room table and sat.

Frank pulled out a notepad and pen from his suit jacket.

"You already know how this goes. There's no need to explain to you what you already know. Let's start with this morning." Frank opened his notepad. "Was there anything off about Destiny today?"

"No, nothing was off. We started off the morning how we usually start off every morning. We got dressed for work and had our morning coffee right here." I touched the table. "Once a week, we decide to go to Meg's Coffee Shop, but we didn't go today."

Frank raised an eyebrow as he scribbled his notes.

"Why didn't you go to Meg's today? Did an altercation happen while you two were at Meg's?"

"No, no. Nothing happened there. We just decided to have coffee here this morning. It's been one of those weeks where it's hard to get out of bed." I shrugged. "We're honestly still in a honeymoon mood."

Frank smiled as he turned his pen over and over in his hand.

"Yeah, I remember those days like it was yesterday."

Frank and his wife, Annalise, had been married for twenty years. I had been around her a few times, and I could see the love that they shared.

He continued with his tirade of questions.

"Did Destiny mention anything to you about something going on at work this past week?"

I thought back to our conversations since we returned to work on Tuesday. The only news Destiny told me was that Mr. Jones, another teacher who taught second grade, broke his foot in a biking accident.

"No, she didn't mention anything happening at work."

Frank rubbed the stubble on his face as he exhaled. He tapped his finger on his lip, deep in thought.

"Did Destiny seem different today?"

I sat back in my chair and stared at the beautiful flower arrangement Destiny painted. The many things that wonderful woman could do amazed me every day.

"No." I looked at Frank. "Everything about Destiny was normal. Everything about our day was normal."

Frank rubbed the balding spot on the top of his head before he asked his next question.

"Does Destiny have any enemies?"

Destiny was the sweetest, most amazing person in this entire world. She'd do anything for anyone that needed help. She cared for her students as if they were her own. The last thing she had was enemies.

"She has no enemies."

Frank scribbled in his notepad before he narrowed his eyes on me. "Are you sure?"

"Yes, I'm sure."

I was adamant about my answer. Destiny didn't do anything to anyone. She didn't bother anyone, so why would anyone want to bother her?

"Wait."

Standing, the chair wooden chair screeched across the floor. I slapped my palm against my forehead and shook my head. I paced the dining room.

"Did you just think of someone that might be a person of interest in Destiny's disappearance?"

"Two people, actually."

Fuming, I balled my hands into fists. How had I not thought about this sooner?

"Names."

Frank's pen hovered over the notepad as he looked at me, waiting for answers.

"Trevor and Melissa Davidson."

Frank furrowed his bushy eyebrows. He tapped his pen on his notepad.

"If I recall correctly, Melissa Davison went to prison two years ago for the murder of Destiny's best friend, Candace, right?"

"Yes, she did," I agreed.

"Trevor went to prison for attempting to cover up Melissa's crime."

"Yes, that's right."

Frank brought up all the facts, yet I could sense he didn't know where I was headed with my philosophy.

"How could they be a person of interest in Destiny's disappearance? They're behind bars."

I chuckled at Frank's confusion as all the pieces came together perfectly.

"Just because you're in prison doesn't mean you don't have access to the outside world."

I stopped pacing and looked at Frank.

"Come on now, we've been doing this long enough to know that people behind bars still have access to people who might do special tasks for them."

"You are going out on a limb with this accusation," Frank said as he closed his notepad and set his pen on top of it.

"I don't think so," I responded.

I paced around the room, completely disgusted with myself for not thinking of this possibility earlier.

Melissa tried to shoot Destiny when she shot Candace, but the gun jammed, and Destiny managed to escape. Trevor tried to murder Destiny once he was able to locate her to protect his wife.

"I'm almost positive one of them knows where Destiny is, or they know who is involved in her disappearance."

"Okay, okay," Frank said after a moment. "First, we will wait to see if we are able to get any fingerprints on Destiny's possessions before we entertain the idea of Trevor and Melissa being involved in Destiny's disappearance."

Stopping in my tracks, my skin grew hot.

"What? Hell no. We can't wait for fingerprints to come back."

Frantically, my eyes roamed my dining room. I stared at the door, willing Destiny to walk in at any second and tell me she was okay.

Sadly, that didn't happen.

"You know we can't wait for the fingerprints. That could take weeks, close to a month, and I'm not waiting that long to question the couple that I know who has a vendetta against my wife."

Frank stood and pushed his chair in.

"We have to follow proper protocol. First, we wait for fingerprints."

Frank might've been listening to what I said, but he wasn't comprehending what came out of my mouth. I had to face it. I had to take matters into my own hands. I needed to get a cell tower triangulation device so I could track any calls that came my way, just to be on the safe side.

"Frank, let me ask you something."

Frank and I walked out of the dining room and headed to the front door.

"What?" he asked as he turned around and looked at me.

"If it was your wife missing, what would you do?" I asked him.

Frank pinched his lips together and looked down. His silence told me everything I needed to know.

"That's what I thought. I'm not waiting for a damn thing to come back. I'll find my wife, even if I have to do it by myself. Nobody, and I mean nobody, is going to hurt her."

Chapter Eight

Destiny

"Destiny, over here."

Looking over my shoulder, I spun around. We were on a beach, and the sun shined bright in the cloudless sky.

Candace stood twenty feet away from me, waving her hand as she smiled. She wore a beautiful, white, flowy dress that went past her knee. Her curly hair touched her shoulders while a sunflower sat behind her right ear. She looked lively and happy.

"Candace," I gasped.

I walked two steps, the feel of the sand in between my toes relaxing. There was nothing better than walking on the beach barefoot. Glancing down, I looked at my red-painted toenails. Smoothing my hands across the soft coral dress I wore, I looked at Candace. Now, she was farther away.

"Candace, where are you going?"

Candace didn't speak. All she did was smile and wave.

With every step I took, Candace would move back at least five feet.

"Candace." Bunching up the bottom of my dress with my hands, I lifted it up so I could move faster. "Please, talk to me."

The brightness of the sun became unbearable. Turning my head, I shielded my eyes before I turned back towards Candace, but she was gone. She had disappeared into thin air, as if she was a figment of my imagination.

Fluttering my eyes open, I stared into the blackness. Everything was still and calm. Thick blackness surrounded me while coolness touched my body. My back ached from the hard, cheap surface I laid on.

Candace. Where had she gone? She felt so close that I could touch her, yet so far away that she disappeared before I had the chance.

Shivering, I looked around, willing my eyes to adjust to the darkness. Where was I? Where was

Zach?

How did I get here? What happened?

Pushing myself up to a sitting position, my head ached, and a dizzy spell washed over me. Clutching my head with both hands, I closed my eyes and breathed through my nose and out through my mouth.

The last thing I remember was leaving Emma's house. Emma, Hannah, and I hugged and gave air kisses before we separated for the night. After that, I had no recollection of anything.

Finally, my eyes adjusted to the darkness. Looking around, I saw metal bars lined in a ten-by-ten square shape around me with one metal door attached. In the far corner, there was a toilet and sink. Jumping up, I stumbled before I ran towards the door and tried to slide it open, but it wouldn't budge.

Banging on the door, I yelled, "Somebody, help me. I'm trapped."

My voice echoed twice, but nobody responded.

Placing my head against the cold metal bars, salty tears slid down my face as I continued to bang, but it was no use. Either nobody was here, or whoever was here didn't care to respond to me.

Why did this happen to me? Who would do this to me? I had no enemies. I respected everyone I encountered and treated them with nothing but respect.

Where was I? I had to be in a constructed jail

of some sort, but where was I? Past the metal bars, I could see a flight of older-looking, rickety stairs that led to above ground. Quite a few places in Sacramento had basements, but surrounding cities also had them as well.

Was I still in Sacramento? Was I in another city? Was I in another state?

I didn't wake up groggy and feeling sluggish for nothing. Something must've happened to me not to remember anything. How long was I asleep? Was I drugged? It sure as hell felt like it.

Zach. Where was Zach? Usually, on my way home, I'd text him and let him know I was en route. I didn't remember if I had texted him when I was on my way home or if I'd forgotten. Sometimes, I'd be so caught up in the moment that I forgot, but I couldn't remember. Why couldn't I remember anything?

What was I missing? Was I knocked out for ten minutes… or a few hours. I racked and racked my brain, but I couldn't remember anything. Would I ever remember?

"Someone, help me," I called out once more as I slapped the door, but my voice came out weak.

Sliding down to the floor, I bawled my eyes out. In this makeshift cage, I was alone and petrified. I didn't know what or who sat on the other side of the metal bars, lying in wait. I didn't know who walked above me, plotting their next evil move. Evidently, this person had to have been a monster for them to hold me against my will in a cold basement with no type of warmth.

All I had on was a pair of blue, distressed jean shorts and a purple top. The shorts or the top provided no type of warmth. The least they could've done was supply me with a blanket to combat this cold environment. They weren't just holding me against my will. They planned to torture me.

Crawling over to the hard bed provided, I laid on it. There was nothing comfortable about it, but it was all I had.

Was this a random act? Had someone watched me for some time now and thought it was the perfect time to prance? I stopped looking over my shoulder when Melissa was sentenced for her part in Candace's murder, and Trevor was sentenced for his part in covering up Candace's murder...

Oh my.

Could I be in this situation because of Melissa and Trevor?

Possibly.

Yes, they were behind bars. Melissa wouldn't see the outside of prison bars for the next twenty-three years if she were able to get parole. Trevor still had eight years to go, but they had access to people on the outside. Melissa seemed to have a lot of power over Trevor, as she convinced him to murder me so that there would be no witnesses. However, Zach derailed Melissa's plan.

I wasn't a detective of any sort, but Zach had done detective work for years. He would get to the bottom of this quickly.

Zach had been protective of me from the moment he found out Candace didn't make it. Thankfully, he didn't allow Trevor to take me into protective custody. Trevor would've offed me once he found out Melissa shot and killed Candace right in front of me.

Thinking about how Candace left this world still caused my heart to ache. Candace was caught in a love triangle that she shouldn't have been in, but love was a drug that Candace couldn't leave alone.

Turning over to my side, the metal springs in the bed dug into my side. Rubbing my hands up and down my arms, I attempted to generate warmth, but it was no use.

When Trevor showed up to the cabin two years ago to get rid of the only witness that could put Melissa behind bars, Zach intercepted and saved me. I knew, without a doubt, that Zach would do everything in his power to save me again. The only difference between this time and the last was that I was not under Zach's care and protection. Zach must apply his skills and find me... wherever I was.

The way Zach had the need to protect me before he fell in love with me was insane. I can only imagine his need to protect me now since I've gone missing. All I can say for the person responsible was that they had an intense force brewing.

A tear slid down my cheek as I closed my

eyes. The thought of my parents hit me hard, a sick feeling settling over me. While I was in protective custody, my parents were worried sick that I was in harm's way. They even wanted me to stay with them while we waited for information on Candace's case. Now, I truly was in harm's way, and I couldn't do anything about it. I couldn't find myself out of this makeshift jail cell. How could I find myself out of this situation? I just knew my parents wouldn't take the news well once Zach informed them that I'd been kidnapped, but he wouldn't be able to hide it for long. My parents and I talked at least twice a week. They would call me if I didn't call them for a few days. I wouldn't want to be on the other side of that phone call.

I had to think happy thoughts. Being down and out, especially when I needed to be the strongest I could be, wouldn't benefit me.

There was a reason I was still alive, sitting in this basement. Whoever kidnapped me needed something from me… or was I bait for Zach? Could this be another person who had absolutely nothing to do with Melissa and Trevor? Could it be someone who was related to another person Zach has put behind bars for a long time? Zach had been responsible for putting a lot of people behind bars over the years. Sometimes, people held grudges. I was a pawn in someone's grudge, but whose?

"Destiny, over here."

Looking over my shoulder, I spun around. We were on a beach, and the sun shined bright in the cloudless sky. The water was crystal clear.

Candace stood fifteen feet away from me, waving her hand as she smiled. She wore a pink bikini. Her curly hair touched her shoulders while a sunflower sat behind her right ear.

"Candace, I'm coming," I called out.

I walked two steps, the feel of the sand in between my toes relaxing. There was nothing better than walking on the beach barefoot. Glancing down, I looked at my red-painted toenails. Smoothing my hands across the soft, lime green one-piece bathing suit I wore, I looked at Candace. Now, she was farther away.

"Candace, where are you going?"

Candace turned around and looked at me. She pointed over her shoulder. "I'm going to get a drink at the bar. Keep up, Destiny. A pina colada is calling my name."

With every step I took, Candace would progress at least five feet.

"Candace," I said. "Slow down."

The brightness of the sun became unbearable. Sliding the sunglasses from the top of my head to over my eyes, the sun became bearable, but the scene in front of my eyes wasn't.

A figure wearing all black appeared behind Candace. They pointed their gun at Candace.

"Candace, watch out," I screamed before I covered my mouth in horror.

Candace turned around, and her eyes opened wide before two loud pops rang out.

My eyes shot open, and I pushed myself up to a sitting position.

"Destiny, sweetheart."

"Oh my gosh," I gasped, catching my breath.

I ran my fingers through my damn hair, trying to control my breathing.

"Sweetheart, are you okay?"

Zach's face swam into my vision. Worry touched every part of his face.

"No." I shook my head. Honestly poured out of me. "No, I'm not."

Zach cupped my face with his hands. "You are safe. Do you understand me?"

Slowly, I nodded. "Yes."

Zach pressed his lips softly against mine before he pressed his forehead against mine. "I told you, I won't ever let anything happen to you. I always have your best interest in mind. Do you believe me?"

"Yes." I looked into his eyes. "I believe you."

"It's been two weeks since we've returned home," Zach pointed out as he rubbed his thumb across my cheek. "The nightmares aren't ceasing. I think it's time you go see someone."

Zach mentioned counseling before we left the cabin. I never, ever considered it as I thought I was strong enough to get through my issues on my own, but I was wrong. I tried for the past two weeks, and I failed miserably. I wasn't as strong as I thought I was.

"It's okay to need help," Zach continued as if he knew exactly what was going through my mind. "Needing counseling doesn't mean that you're weak. Trust me, you are the strongest person I've ever met." Zach pinched my cheek, and I smiled. "You'll learn healthy ways to deal with the issues you suffer from."

"Okay, I'll do counseling."

My eyes shot open, my heart pounding loudly in my ears. I stared into the still blackness. Sadly, Zach couldn't wake me up from this nightmare that I lived. I was stuck in this nightmare until I clawed my way out... or Zach rescued me, whichever came first.

Chapter Nine

Zach

I sipped my coffee and winced as the hot liquid burned my lip. This was my third cup in the past two hours, and it wouldn't be the last. I placed the carafe back on the burner before I walked to the dining table and sat.

The yard finally cleared of all police personnel a little after midnight. Once the crime scene tape was removed, I jumped into my truck and drove.

I had no destination in mind, but I had to search for Destiny. I didn't even know where to start, but I refused to be a sitting duck. There was no information on what car to look for since none of our neighbors had seen or heard anything out of sorts. Another issue was that nobody in the area had outdoor cameras that could have spotted the getaway vehicle.

Installing cameras around the house had been my priority since Destiny moved in, but Destiny decided against it since we were in the market to buy another house. Her philosophy was that there was no reason to install a camera if we moved right after finding our forever home.

We were supposed to attend another open house this morning, but we couldn't make it. Making that call this morning to cancel the open house for our potential forever home made my heart ache. If things hadn't taken a turn for the worse last night, we'd have made that visit.

Closing my eyes, I rubbed my temples and exhaled. Sleeping last night was nearly impossible after I returned home after hours of searching. No matter how much I wanted to stay awake, willing my wife to walk through the front door, my heavy eyelids won around four in the morning, and I had no choice but to fall asleep.

Something jolted me awake at seven this morning. Physically, my body was exhausted, but I didn't have time to rest. I could survive off three hours and loads of coffee.

"Is there anything I can do?" Jake asked. He

cradled his own cup of coffee.

Last night, after I spoke with Emma, she informed Jake about what was happening. Once he sobered up enough where he wasn't puking all over himself, he had Emma drive him over. So, he'd been with me since two this morning. Besides asking if I was okay, Jake stayed quiet and listened. He offered an ear when I needed to vent. He offered a shoulder when I needed to cry. Jake was the best friend that I could've asked for.

"No." I sipped my coffee. "You've done more than enough by being here."

Jake stood and poured himself another cup of coffee.

"What's on the agenda today?"

I tapped my fingers on the table.

"Well, I have to make some visits to the prison today. I know Trevor and Melissa know something."

Jake raised his eyebrow. He sat next to me before he took a tentative sip.

"Isn't that what Frank should be doing? Since he is in charge of Destiny's case?"

Scoffing, I replied, "Frank's way of trying to deal with my wife's disappearance doesn't sit well with me. So, I'm doing what I need to do. I've already put in my request for FMLA. While he tries to go through things the *protocol* way, I'm going to go visit what I'm sure is the root cause of Destiny's disappearance."

"Are you sure this has anything to do with them?"

Confused, I asked, "What do you mean, am I sure?"

Jake shrugged.

"You were a detective for years. There could've been anyone from your past responsible for this. Marriage records are public records. Anyone could've seen that you married Destiny and decided to act because you finally had someone in your life that you loved besides you, me and your mother."

Jake tossed in a wink when he referred to himself.

"No." Shaking my head, I said, "This just feels personal. How Destiny's items were scattered in the front yard, the person responsible was sending a message."

"Care to explain that message?" Jake asked as he sat back and sipped his coffee.

"I would …" I began, but I checked the time on my watch. "But we have to leave. I have to drive an hour away."

"Who are you going to visit today?" Jake asked as he stood and walked to the cabinet.

He grabbed two styrofoam cups.

"Trevor." Jake handed me a cup, and I poured my coffee into it and placed my cup in the sink. "I think he's easier to crack, the weaker link of the two."

"I hope he tells you exactly what you need to know." Jake poured his coffee into his cup. "I can't wait for my sister to come back home."

Jake started referring to Destiny as his sister

from the second she moved into the house with me. I knew deep down that I wanted to marry her from the second I held her in my arms for the first time. I didn't want to admit it to myself, from my previous experiences of loving someone that hurt me deeply.

I just knew it felt right, getting to know Destiny as herself outside of the cabin. We were forced into seclusion for her safety, and outside of the cabin, she was the same person I fell in love with. That's when I knew I was correct in my decision to want to marry her.

"I can't wait, either."

Destiny's presence made me feel safe and secure in my own little way. Without her, I didn't feel like myself. I needed my other half.

As I drove Jake home, the lull of country music played in the background. Jake could sense I wasn't in the talking mood, so he stayed silent. I tapped my fingers on the steering wheel as I thought about Destiny.

I prayed and prayed she was still alive, not lying in a ditch somewhere. Something within me told me she was still alive, but I had to prepare myself for anything. I had to expect the unexpected.

"Will you call me later?" Jake asked as I pulled into his driveway.

"Yeah, I'll call you."

Looking off in the distance, I took a deep breath and slowly exhaled. Destiny not only taught me how to love again, but she also taught me how to defuse my stress. Sadly, it wasn't working right now. The only thing that could defuse my stress was Destiny's presence.

"Zach."

Pulling my eyes away from the garage door, I looked over at Jake.

"Yes."

Jake shook his head. He ran his hand through his hair.

"I'm worried about, man. I've called your name like five times. You're out of it."

Did he really call me that many times?

"I didn't hear you, I'm sorry." Checking the time on the radio, I exhaled. "I have to get going. I'll reach out later."

Placing the truck in reverse, I waited for Jake to close the passenger door.

"Are you sure you don't need me to go with you?"

"No." I looked forward. "I need to do this on my own."

"Please, be safe. Think rational. Don't do anything that'll jeopardize your character or the advancement of this case."

Jake and his many words of wisdom. Seriously, I couldn't ask for a better best friend.

"I won't."

Jake gave a sympathetic smile before he closed the door.

The men's prison was forty-five minutes away. I'd make sure I'd get there in less time.

Thirty-five minutes later, I parked in the

prison's parking lot. I knew the drive well since I've had to come here during the years I was a detective to question several men behind bars. Contrary to popular belief, people behind bars had just as much power behind bars as when they were in the free world. All it took was the right connections in the free world.

Walking through the prison doors, a feeling of déjà vu washed over me. The last time I had walked through these prison doors, I had to question a suspect about his ex-wife's attempted murder. Turned out, he had hired a hitman on the outside, talking in code during his calls, to set the entire sting up. He had communicated with an undercover cop the entire time, offering him twenty thousand dollars to kill his ex-wife. When I confronted him with all the evidence we built up, his eyes widened with shock. He knew he would be charged with the attempted murder of his ex-wife.

After I informed the attendant whom I came to visit and showed my badge, I was escorted to an investigation room. I wasn't there on official business through my job. I was there on official business concerning my wife. Using my badge to get things down was a necessity.

Tapping my fingers on the mental table, I looked around the room. One fluorescent light shined from above, flickering every so often. The room smelled of stale coffee and cleaning bleach.

The door creaked open, and a sturdy, muscular, tall, armed guard walked in, guiding a shackled Trevor.

Trevor had a bit more muscle on him now than the last time I saw him. His facial hair had grown in, making him look at least ten years older and nearly unrecognizable. He was overdue for a haircut.

When Trevor looked at me, his eyes widened.

"We'll, I'll be damned. I never thought Miller would grace me with his presence."

I nodded at Trevor. "I could say the same, Davidson."

Calling each other by our last names nearly brought me back to when we were coworkers. Sadly, he allowed his wife to ruin his life by taking him down the wrong path in life. No longer was he a police officer but a prison inmate.

The guard sat Trevor in the metal chair across the room from me. The chair screeched as it slid across the tiled floor.

"I'll be right outside if you need me," the guard said before he walked out the door.

Silence didn't sit long before Trevor spoke. He motioned around the room. "I'm honestly surprised to see you. Who do I owe the honor of you visiting me?"

Sitting back, I analyzed Trevor. Appearance-wise, he looked like the same Trevor I had the chance to get to know, but prison had a way of changing people.

"I'm here to speak with you about Destiny."

Trevor sat back in his chair and crossed his

left leg over his right.

"What's going on with Destiny?" Calm and collective energy oozed off his body. "Did you two finally break it off…"

"Destiny is my wife, and she has gone missing."

Trevor covered his mouth with his hands, causing the metal wrapped around his wrists to jingle.

"Destiny's your wife now?" Trevor looked amazed. "Wow. I never thought she meant that much to you. I've missed so much being behind bars."

Scoffing, I looked away from Trevor. Blood boiling, I balled my hands into fists. He acknowledged the first half of my sentence but completely disregarded the second half.

"Let's cut the bullshit, all right?"

Trevor raised his eyebrows.

"I didn't come here to catch up with you on what has happened in my life."

Running my hands over my matted ponytail, I almost regretted the fact that I didn't bother doing my hair this morning, but the only brush I thought to grab was my toothbrush.

"I sure as hell can care less what's going on in yours. If I were here to catch up with you on how prison life was treating you, we wouldn't be in this interrogation room. We'd be in the common room, playing a game of cards while you snacked on a soda and a bag of chips."

Trevor stared at me with wide eyes.

"What's going on?"

"Destiny's gone missing."

Trevor gasped. "What the hell happened?"

"I don't know." I sat up and stared him in the eyes. "That's why I'm here."

Trevor pointed at himself. "You think I have something to do with this?"

Shrugging, I responded, "I don't know, you tell me."

Trevor shook his head several times. "Oh, hell no. You aren't going to pin this on me." He looked around the investigation room before he looked back at me. "How would I be responsible for Destiny's disappearance? I'm stuck behind bars for the next eight years."

"You might be stuck behind bars, but that doesn't mean you don't have access to anyone on the outside. You know just as much as I do that people behind bars can make things happen on the outside with the snap of their fingers."

Trevor leaned forward, placed his elbows on the table, and tapped his fingers.

"I don't have anyone," Trevor began. "My parents never approved of my relationship with Melissa. They always thought she was toxic for me, but what could I say." Trevor smiled. "I was in love with her and chose Melissa over my parents."

I wasn't here for story time, but if it led me to discover more about what could've possibly happened to Destiny, I was ready to listen with open ears.

"Once I helped Melissa and got twisted up in attempting to cover up her crime, my parents completely disowned me once I was sentenced. My so-called friends visited me once when I first came here, and they have yet to return. I never knew what it felt like to be alone until I watched those metal gates close."

Watching the way Trevor's eyes moved while he spilled his feelings and emotions to me, almost made me believe him. Almost. Some people were great at masking their true feelings and emotions. I'd seen it over the years, and this was nothing different than I was used to.

Leaning forward, I spoke sternly. "I know you still have ill feelings towards my wife."

Trevor opened his mouth and said, "But—"

Interrupting him, I held my index finger up and said, "Let me finish."

He nodded and continued to listen.

"Even though she's not the reason you are in this situation, it's your wife's fault. I know you hold resentment towards her for you rotting in a jail cell for the next eight years."

"Wow." Trevor gasped as he placed his hand over his heart. "Tell me how you really feel."

Standing up forcefully, my chair screeched across the tile floor. All I saw was red.

"Don't make me jack your…"

"Okay, okay." Trevor held his hands out, fear dancing in his eyes. "I'm sorry."

I had him exactly where I wanted him to be.

"Tell me what you know."

I slammed my hands against the table, no doubt drawing the attention of the guard outside.

The door opened, and the guard peeked inside. His eyes bounced back and forth between Trevor and me.

"Is everything okay in here?" he asked, running his hand across the taser on his belt.

"Yes," Trevor answered a bit too quickly.

The guard looked at me, waiting for my response.

"Everything is fine."

He gave us one last look before he closed the door.

"I am not lying to you." Trevor stared me directly in the eyes. "I don't know anything about Destiny's disappearance."

Tapping my foot against the tile, I asked him the million-dollar question.

"Do you think your wife is behind all of this?"

Trevor exhaled slowly. He twisted his mouth and rubbed his chin before he answered.

"Honestly, I'm not sure. I haven't spoken to Melissa since I came here. I've always known Melissa to hold a grudge, but that doesn't mean she's the only one in this world who could hold a grudge."

"What are you saying?" I asked.

"I'm saying, I think it's possible that someone from your past, besides Melissa, could be responsible. You and Frank have placed a lot of people behind bars. You two are great detectives. Melissa cannot be the only person with a grudge."

I hate to say it, but Trevor might not be wrong.

"If someone held a grudge against me, why would they go after my wife instead of me?"

"You might suffer a little bit if you're kidnapped, but tell me, how do you feel with Destiny being kidnapped?"

My breath escaped me. "Like the world has come to an end."

"Do you seriously believe Melissa is behind all of this?" Trevor asked.

"I'm not sure about anything anymore." Standing, I pushed my chair in. "Deep in my gut, I think she's responsible. It's time to pay Melissa a visit."

Chapter Ten

Destiny

"Destiny."

Turning around, I saw Zach across the room. We were in an unfamiliar room, crowded with people.

"Zach, I'm over here," I called out.

His eyes roamed around the room. He looked over me as if I wasn't even there.

"Destiny, where are you?" Zach sounded frantic.

I pushed myself past the people blocking my path to Zach. He was within my reach. Reaching out, I tried to touch him, but my hand went through his body.

Recoiling my hand, I gasped. Zach's eyes danced over me before he walked through me.

Was I invisible?

He called my name once more before he disappeared.

Fluttering my eyes open, I stared into the darkness. Blinking my eyes several times, I hoped and prayed the darkness would turn to light and I'd be at home, waking up in my own bed.

When I opened my eyes once more, darkness loomed. I wasn't at home. I was still in this hell hole, being held like a dirty prisoner.

I pushed myself up to a sitting position.

What was up with these visions? Or were they dreams? Not only had I experienced two similar dreams about Candace, with some minor detail changes, but now I had a dream about Zach?

Did these dreams really happen? Or was it just my imagination playing tricks on me?

I ran my fingers through my messy bun as my head ached. There was no telling how long I'd been here. I could've been here for a day or three days. Nothing around could give me an idea of a time stamp.

Swallowing, my throat ached with dryness. Oh, what I would do for a glass of ice-cold water or some delicious, sweet tea. I dragged my index finger across my chapped lips, yearning for anything that resembled an edible liquid to touch them.

My stomach rumbled with hunger. Oh, what I'd do for a nice medium rare steak. Hell, I'd be perfectly content scarfing down Brussels sprouts, my least favorite food item to eat.

I needed food. Most importantly, I needed water.

As my eyes adjusted more to the dark, I made my move. Scooting to the cold floor, I heard a loud sound. My heart was pounding in my chest, and I stilled my movements and looked up. Was that a bang? Or did I imagine it? I chalked it up to my imagination.

Crawling around, sand stuck to my hand. Before placing me here, the least they could've done was sweep or vacuum the area. I couldn't wait until I could find myself out of this place. It was horrible, dirty, creepy and cold. Surprisingly, I wasn't sure how I was able to sleep, but my body must've been exhausted.

My hand smacked into something hard. Narrowing my eyes, I noticed a plastic plate and a beat-up cup.

Sitting on my butt, I grabbed the cup with both hands and gulped down the water. I didn't care if the cup was clean or if the water in the cup was tap, I needed to quench my thirst. Sadly, there wasn't enough water to do that.

I grabbed the sandwich from the plate and I

took a bite. The bread was hard and dry, and I couldn't make out the type of lunch meat. All I knew was that the sandwich was the worst I'd ever had. Gagging, I scarfed down the sandwich. Bringing my knees up to my chest, I placed my head in my lap, closed my eyes and rocked, willing myself not to allow the sandwich to come back up and make an awful appearance.

Raising my head from my lap, I stared at the metal door. I couldn't imagine how I was still alive unless this person wanted to torture me before they took my life. That was the only thing that made sense. They had me in a cold basement with no blankets, provided nearly inedible food and water, and I was in the dark.

Was I going crazy? I kept seeing Candace and Zach. Some of these flashes that I had seemed to have occurred before, and some parts hadn't. Was that the purpose of having me here? For me to slowly go crazy and lose myself? Who would want this for me? Who hated me enough to do this?

The more I thought about it, the more I pointed my finger at Melissa. There was no doubt in my mind that Trevor might be upset about being behind bars, but he didn't seem like that type of person. Trevor owned up to his actions in court.

Melissa, on the other hand, hadn't. Melissa was the only person that held a grudge against me. In her eyes, I was the reason she and her husband were behind bars.

Even though it was their actions that they did on their own free will that placed them behind bars, I was still to blame. It was easier to blame someone else than take responsibility for her actions. Maturing mentally would make her understand that I wasn't the issue here.

Since they were both behind bars, that could only mean someone on the outside was doing the dirty work. If I had learned something when Trevor came to the cabin in the middle of the night, it was to cover up Melissa's mistakes. He didn't want his wife to go down for the murder of his mistress. Trevor didn't seem like a vindictive person, but Melissa did.

I wasn't great at putting the pieces together like Zach, but I had learned a thing or two from him since he came into my life.

One other thing I had learned, Zach had already put his detective skills to use. He would do anything for me, and I knew he'd go to the ends of the earth to find me, protect me and make me feel safe.

I remembered the day he proposed to me. It was a beautiful, sunny Sunday. Two days earlier on Friday, Zach had told me he wanted to take me to the cabin for the weekend. He surprised me with the information as soon as I stepped in the front door when I came home from work.

"Pack some clothes. We are getting away for the weekend," Zach called out as I closed the door behind me.

Throwing a smile over my shoulder, I hung

my keys on the wall and kicked my shoes off. "Oh, I love the spontaneous nature. What's the occasion?"

Zach shrugged as I walked into the living room.

"You've been working hard."

He stood, walked over to me and wrapped his arms around me. He nuzzled my neck with his nose, giving me goosebumps and sending shivers up my spine.

"I think you deserve a mini getaway."

I couldn't argue with that. "Okay, where are we going?"

Zach grabbed my hands, opened his mouth and hesitated.

Raising an eyebrow, I leaned my weight on one foot. When Zach hesitated, it meant he didn't know how to say what was on his mind.

"Is it a top secret?" I asked.

Zach chuckled before he rubbed the stubble on his chin.

"We're going to my cabin."

The smile on my face disintegrated. That was the last place I wanted to go, but I wouldn't object. Maybe Zach knew something I didn't.

The trip he planned was spur the moment. It had been months since I stepped foot in the cabin, and I hadn't planned on doing it tomorrow. Mentally preparing myself would've suffice, but I didn't argue with Zach.

Zach and I had some wonderful memories to cherish there. That's where we had our first kiss, made love for the first time, and told each other we loved the other. Even though I have wonderful memories there, I had one horrible memory there that trumped all the wonderful. The last memory I had being there was nearly being killed by Trevor.

The cabin was my safe space when I needed protection after Candace's death, but I didn't view it that way after that space was tainted. Now, Zach invited me there for the weekend. How could I step foot in there?

Well, I managed to do it. I placed one shaky foot in front of the other. Somehow, the cabin atmosphere didn't set me off, though. A nostalgic feeling settled over me while we were there. The feeling reminded me of those days when I began falling for Zach through my pain and sorrow.

After we arrived Saturday morning after stopping to have breakfast at a hole-in-the-wall restaurant, we washed up before we made Zach's grandmother's secret chocolate chip cookie recipe. We hung out in the living room while watching movies before walking around the cabin as the day turned to dusk.

Sunday after lunch, Zach grabbed my hand, placed his other hand on my lower back, and led me to the front door.

"Where are we going?"

Zack opened the door. "Let's go sit on the porch."

Zach led me to the porch swing he had installed last month. We sat together, and I snuggled under his arm.

He slowly kicked his foot and rocked us on the swing. As we rocked together, our future flashed before my eyes. I saw us sitting on this porch, gray-haired while our grandchildren ran around the front yard, talking and laughing together.

"What are you smiling about?" Zach asked me.

Should I tell him? Should I keep it to myself? What if he wasn't on this level of thinking? What if all he could see me for was a girlfriend?

I opened my mouth, and nothing came out.

"Speechless, huh?" Zach winked as he grabbed my chin and rubbed his thumb across it. There was nothing that this man could do that wouldn't make my body react in such a way.

All I could do was nod.

"Well, I need your speechlessness to go away for a few moments because..."

He slowed the swing, stood and dropped down on one knee in front of me.

Gasping, my heart pounded. Covering my mouth with both hands, all the doubts that entered my mind just a few moments ago disappeared.

He reached into his pocket and pulled out a black ring box. He grabbed my left hand and kissed the back of it.

"I never, ever thought I would love again until you came into my life." He paused, took a deep breath, and continued. "The moment I laid eyes on you, I knew there was something about you that I couldn't get enough of. It's safe to say the time I have spent with you has been the best time of my life."

Tears fell from Zach's eyes. Reaching out, I wiped his tears away as my own tears blinded my vision and touched my cheeks.

"I've been holding off proposing for months. I've had this ring for four months but had to get the timing and location right."

I couldn't believe what I heard. How did I question if he saw me more than a girlfriend and he had already purchased the engagement ring four months ago?

"Destiny Auburn Taylor, will you marry me?" Zach opened the box, and a white gold, heart-shaped ring sparkled.

"Yes, yes, yes."

Zach slipped the ring onto my finger before we both stood. I wrapped my arms around his neck, and he wrapped his arms around my waist, lifting me off the ground.

Zach kissed me, slipping his tongue into my mouth.

"I can't wait until I walk down the aisle and say, 'I do' to you," I whispered against Zach's lips.

"We can get married tomorrow in our living room, next week in Paris, or we can get married in a year with all our family and friends." Zach kissed my forehead. "Whatever makes you happy."

So many options Zach gave me, yet having all of our friends and family together sounded the best.

I ran my fingers through Zach's hair.

"What made you decide to wait so many months to come here and propose?"

"Ever since we arrived home, whenever I'd mention visiting the cabin, you would become tense. I knew I needed to do something so amazing here that you would be content to spend some time coming back here. So, proposing to you right here, right now, was the best decision I've ever made. The last, most amazing memory you'll have here is being proposed to."

A noise from above broke me from my memory. I looked up into the darkness, waiting for the sound to happen again, but it didn't.

I ran my index finger across my ring finger and touched my engagement ring and wedding band. Thankfully, whoever kidnapped me didn't take my rings from me. Not only would I be scared out of my mind, but I'd also be completely heartbroken. These rings were a symbol of the commitment I made to Zach.

How did I go from marrying the love of my life about a week ago to sitting in the dark, at an unknown location, waiting for him to rescue me from wherever I was held hostage?

I tried my hardest to hold in the tears that threatened to appear, but it was useless. Tears cascaded down my face, and my chest ached with sorrow. This was not how I imagined spending the first few months as a newlywed.

I could only imagine how he felt right now if I

felt this lousy being away from Zach. I'm sure he didn't know anything, such as if I were dead or alive or if I were still in Sacramento or on the other side of the United States. So many what-ifs, yet no answers.

Rubbing my hands up and down my arms, I attempted to generate warmth. My sandwich didn't sit well in my stomach, but I had to keep it down. I needed all the strength I could muster from the food my kidnapper fed me if I planned to survive.

I just hoped Zach took care of himself. Knowing him, he survived off several cups of coffee with little to no sleep while he followed up on every small detail that might lead him to my location. He wouldn't stop until he found me… or my body.

Zach only changed positions in the police department for my sanity. With passion, he loved being a detective. His job was to help everyone find closure, whether the outcome was positive or negative. My trauma influenced him to change his career, and I couldn't help but feel horrible about it.

How could I allow my trauma to change his career? Did that make me a horrible fiancé, now wife?

Placing my head in my hands, I cried silent tears. Being in this dark, cold place had me losing my sanity.

Pushing myself to a standing position, I walked over to the gate. I tugged on the handle with all my might, but it didn't budge.

Banging on the gate, I screamed out in pain.

"Someone, get me out of here," I yelled as I grabbed the bars and shook them, but the bars didn't even move. "Get me the hell out of here."

I didn't know how long I waited for an answer or for someone to walk down and come rescue me.

Slowly, I dropped to the ground. I had used all the energy I could muster.

There was one thing I knew, I needed to get out of here. I needed to get out of here now.

Chapter Eleven

Zach

Grabbing my cup, I raised my shaky hand and took a sip of my fourth cup of coffee of the morning.

I wasn't sure if I was shaking from the caffeine I inhaled around the clock or the lack of sleep. It didn't matter, though. I had to get myself together.

There was no chance in hell I would give up on my search. Destiny was out there somewhere.

I could feel it in my heart. I had a gut feeling that she was alive. The real question was, where was she? All I had to do was locate her.

Taking another sip of my coffee, I leaned against the counter.

My trip to visit Trevor didn't result in too much information. On my drive back home, I finally came to terms with the fact that Trevor wasn't responsible for Destiny's disappearance. I could see it in his eyes.

Even though Trevor might not have anything to do with it, that didn't check Melissa off my list. Melissa was always number one on my suspect list. Trevor was a close second. He would've been the easiest one to crack if he was involved. Since I got nowhere, taking that route, it was time to pay Melissa a visit.

After I downed my cup of coffee, I grabbed my badge, keys, and a bottle of water.

Next stop: The women's prison.

Starting the truck, I didn't give it a second to warm up before I backed out of the driveway. I was on a time crunch, and the prison was an hour's drive.

Tonight would officially make it forty-eight hours since Destiny went missing. The first forty-eight hours are crucial in every criminal investigation. After those forty-eight hours, the chances of finding Destiny would dwindle tremendously.

It felt like months since I last cupped her face and kissed her sweet lips. It felt like forever since

I looked into her sweet, innocent brown eyes and saw our future. There's no way I could spend the rest of my life without Destiny. I had spent the first thirty-one years of my life without her. I refused to spend the rest of my life without her.

I could thank Destiny's parents for bringing her into this world. Without them, my soulmate wouldn't exist. I could thank Destiny's stepdad for raising her as his own daughter. I hoped they wouldn't reach out until I got Destiny home. The last thing I needed was for them to worry. They did enough worrying when she was in protective custody. I couldn't break their hearts with this information. All three of them.

The first time Destiny and I went on a date outside of the cabin was unimaginable. I asked her to come up with the agenda, and she came up with the most unorthodox date imaginable.

Destiny woke up on a cheerful Saturday morning and walked into the dining room. I sat in the dining room with a cup of coffee and looked up, happy to see her beautiful face.

Last night, Destiny hadn't woken up with any nightmares. It was progress from the last three nights in a row that I had to cradle her in my arms and comfort her. She surprised me so much last night I woke up in the middle of the night to make sure she was okay. She was sound asleep, with her curly hair splayed across the pillow. She was a real-life goddess, and I was lucky to call her my girlfriend.

She sauntered over to me and placed her

hands on my shoulder.

"I'm taking you on a date today," she whispered.

Looking over my shoulder, I asked, "Are you asking, or are you telling me?"

She rubbed my shoulders in a circular motion. Moving my head from side to side, Destiny responded with, "Zach, can I take you on a date?"

"Hm." I tapped my finger on my lips. "Let me think about it."

Playfully, she slapped my arm before she folded her arms across her chest. I tugged my eyes away from her breasts, meeting her eyes.

"You know I'm only kidding." Taking another sip of my coffee, I stood, faced her and wrapped my arms around her waist. "Where are we going?"

"Oh no." She removed my hands from around her waist before standing on her tippy toes and kissing my nose's tip. "You won't find that out until we arrive." She looked me up and down, her eyes sparkling with happiness. "Get dressed. You'll want to wear something that'll keep you cool."

She kissed me once more before she walked out of the dining room.

Destiny ended up taking me to a zoo I had never visited. We had a ton of fun while we walked around and saw all the animals. After our visit to the zoo, Destiny took us to a massage parlor to have a couples massage. It was my first massage, and it surely wouldn't be my last.

Lastly, we ended our date night eating Pad Thai at a wonderful hole-in-the-wall Thai restaurant. That was the best date I had ever been on.

Squeezing the steering wheel tight enough to turn my hands ash white, I pulled into the women's prison guest parking lot. The trip here went a lot smoother than I expected at this time of day.

It had been years since I last visited this prison. The last time I was here, I worked on a unique case. A woman had been accused of murdering three men over the course of two weeks. There was substantial evidence built up against her.

I came to investigate her quite a few times. Our conversations were pleasant, considering she knew how to twist the narrative around. After receiving her favorite coffee drink, she gave me a little more information each visit.

She was calculated with everything she had done. The very last time, she finally admitted to me how she carried out all three murders.

She specifically picked out each man while she sat at the local bar. While she puffed on her cigar and sipped on her whiskey sour, she calculated every interaction. After she convinced them to leave the bar with her, she put her plan into action and killed them. One by one.

After showing my badge and signing in, a guard walked me to an interrogation room. The room reeked of antiseptic, causing my nose to wiggle and burn.

Five minutes passed before a woman guard guided a shackled Melissa into the room. Her head was held low, and she walked in lazily, her shoulders hung low. Her hair had grown quite a few inches since the last time I saw her.

Looking up, her eyes widened when she noticed me.

The guard sat Melissa down in the metal chair across from me. The whole time the guard situated Melissa, she stared at me, a devious look in her eyes. The last thing the guard did before she walked out was handcuff Melissa to the table.

Once the guard exited the room, she examined her wrists. She didn't even acknowledge that I was in the room with her.

If I could sense anything from the path of how our interaction was going, I knew this conversation would be negative.

"Hello, Melissa," I said after two minutes of silence.

Dragging her eyes away from her wrists, she looked at me and nodded her head. "What's up, Zach. Long time no see. How have you been?"

Nonchalant was going to be her approach. This would be harder than I thought.

"Not so great, actually," I answered truthfully.

She looked me in the eyes, her green eyes never wavering.

"Something serious must've happened for you to come here." She smirked as she motioned around the room. "Honestly, this was the last visit I ever expected."

"Yes, something serious has happened." Leaning forward, I placed my elbows on the table. "Destiny has been kidnapped."

Melissa gasped as her eyes widened. Metal clinked as she attempted to cover her mouth with her hands, but her being handcuffed to the table prevented it. Surprisingly, she showed genuine concern. "Are you sure?"

"Yes, I'm sure."

Melissa's eyes darted around the room.

"Do you know anything about this?" I asked.

"How do you know she was kidnapped?" Melissa leaned back in her chair, completely ignoring my question. "She could've left of her own free will." She shrugged. "I would if I had to deal with you."

Scrunching my eyes, I was taken back. Melissa not only insulted my intelligence, but she insulted me. I would be the bigger person and ignore her slick remarks.

"Yes, I know she didn't leave of her free will. All her belongings were scattered in the front yard. It was obvious there was a struggle."

"Destiny's gone, so what? What does any of this have to do with me?"

Taking a deep breath, I willed myself not to react. One of the first things I learned when I became a detective was not to allow my personal feelings to get in the way of an investigation. Since this case was personal, that was one lesson I couldn't follow, no matter how hard I tried.

"Well, I tried to be the good cop in this investigation, but it doesn't seem like I'm getting anywhere doing that." Straightening my posture, I narrowed my eyes to her. "I know you have something to do with Destiny's disappearance. Where the hell is my wife?"

"Wife?" Melissa chuckled as she smiled. "Destiny is your wife now, huh? Wow, the things I have missed while being in this hellhole."

"Where is Destiny?" I asked again, my voice growing stern. I had to ignore her cockiness and lack of feelings she held within for Destiny. She was a cold-hearted killer.

"How could I have something to do with Destiny's disappearance?" She motioned around the room. "I've been stuck in here for the past two years. The guards won't allow me to walk outside freely. Trust me, I've asked one... or a million times."

"You and I both know there are ways around that. I know there must be someone on the outside who would do anything for you."

Melissa pursed her lips. "Care to tell me? I would love to know. The last person that truly would do anything for me was Trevor. He couldn't even do that right, so now we both sit behind bars."

"Melissa, stop the bullshit. Okay?"

Melissa smiled devilishly. "No, it's just getting started."

Growling under my breath, I balled my hands into fists. This was a woman I dealt with, but I wished that with everything I had, it was a man I could pummel to the ground.

"Where is Destiny?" I asked once more.

"I have no idea what you're talking about," Melissa said in a monotone voice. "Now that you mention it, I do have people on the outside who would do anything for me."

"Who might that be?"

Willing the answer to slip off the tip of her tongue, I grabbed my notepad and pen out of my pocket, prepared to write down the name of the person I needed to contact.

She pushed air out of her cheeks before she cracked a smile.

"You're the detective. Isn't it your job to figure that out?"

My pen fell out of my grasp, landing on the table. Needing something to do with my hands, anything so I wouldn't do something that would put me in jail, I rubbed the stubble on my chin.

"I can't believe you've admitted to me that you know who is behind Destiny's disappearance."

"No, no, no." Melissa shook her head and wagged her index finger at me. She tossed a wink at me, taunting me. "I didn't admit anything. That is your assumption based on what I stated."

Melissa and her stubborn antics. This woman would never change, even if change slapped her in the face several times or it was served up to her on a silver platter.

"Is Trevor behind all of this?"

Trevor told me he wasn't responsible, but Melissa would at least tell me the truth about Trevor.

Melissa rolled her eyes. "You don't listen very well, do you? Trevor didn't successfully get rid of Destiny the first time. Why do you think I would trust him to get rid of her a second time?"

Melissa talked in circles. She basically admitted to me that someone in her world was behind Destiny's disappearance; she just didn't tell me specifically who it was.

"If you don't tell me who is responsible..."

"You'll do what?" Melissa asked, interrupting me. "You can't touch me. You can't do anything to me. I'm practically untouchable."

Slapping my hands on the table, I stood.

"This conversation is over."

Stuffing my notepad and pen back into my pocket, I walked to the door. Coming here seemed like the biggest mistake I could've made, but Melissa gave me half the information I needed in the most horrific way possible. She played with fire. That was a deadly game of cat and mouse. Even though I should've been the cat, I was essentially the mouse. Melissa played with me with her paws.

"Wait."

My hand hovered over the doorknob. Everything in me told me not to acknowledge her anymore, but I didn't listen to the small voice in the back of my head. I turned to look over my shoulder.

"You mean, this was a conversation?" Melissa's eyes widened.

Staying silent, I didn't answer her question. I just waited for what else I knew would come out of her mouth.

"I could've sworn you wanted this to be an interrogation, but you didn't do the best job at interrogating me."

Scoffing, I rolled my eyes and shook my head. The little voice in my head was correct.

"Maybe you should go into another field. The police field doesn't seem to work for you."

"You'll see me again," I answered, ignoring her tyrant behavior.

She thrived in making me feel powerless.

"No matter how many days, months, or years pass by, it'll be too soon," Melissa answered before she wiggled her finger at me.

Without another response, I walked out of the interrogation room.

Someone in Melissa's world was behind Destiny's disappearance. Her cockiness dug into my skin, but in this industry, tough skin was a must. All I had to do was look into her history and see what could be found. Nothing, and I mean nothing, would stop me from finding out who Melissa's right-hand man was on the outside. I'd put my life on it.

Chapter Twelve

Destiny

My eyes shot open. I moved them from side to side, trying to find some light but darkness surrounded me. I didn't know what it felt like to be in the light again. I craved the light with everything in me.

I tried to lift my arm, but I was too weak. My stomach ached with hunger pains. My limbs throbbed from coolness.

Opening my mouth to call out for help for the

hundredth time, I snapped it shut. My mouth was as dry as the Sahara Desert. Calling out for help proved useless, but I held onto a sliver of hope that someone would help. I wasn't sure how long I'd been in this basement, but it felt like I'd been here for months.

A clatter from above startled me. With all my might, I pushed myself to a sitting position, anticipating the next noise that would sound.

Rubbing my finger across my lip, I closed my eyes and exhaled.

Opening my eyes, I stared into Emma's neighbor's yard across the street. The streetlights had just come on and highlighted the yard well. My arms were wrapped around someone, and they patted my back.

Once we separated, I smiled into Emma's face as we grabbed each other's hands and gave them a squeeze.

"I need some loving as well, don't forget about me," came from over my shoulder.

Hannah wrapped her arms around me, and I basked in the love I received from my friends. She rubbed my back before our hug ended.

I grabbed one of Emma's hands and one of Hannah's hands.

"I love you two so much." I looked back and forth in between the two of them.

"Are you okay?" Hannah analyzed me as she raised an eyebrow. "You're telling us this like something is going to happen."

"Yeah, is something going to happen that you

didn't tell us over dinner?" Emma asked.

Shaking my head, I responded, "No, nothing is going to happen," I reassured them. "I just don't tell you two that enough."

"How about we make a pact," Emma suggested.

"What kind of pact?" Hannah asked.

"We tell one another that we love them every day."

"That sounds like the perfect pact," I agreed.

Emma, Hannah and I hugged before Hannah, and I walked to our vehicles.

Emma stood in the doorway waving as Hannah and I backed out of the driveway and headed separate ways.

Drumming my fingers on the steering wheel to the beat of the pop song that played, I drove with a smile that wouldn't waver. Even though I knew we were close, tonight's discussion just further solidified how amazing and strong our friendship was.

Glancing at my purse in the passenger seat, I cursed under my breath. I was so caught up with Emma and Hannah that I forgot to text Zach, saying that I was on my way home. It wasn't the first time I had done it, and it surely wouldn't be the last. I would text him, but after I sent a quick text to him previously while at a stop light, Zach informed me that it was unsafe. I would just wait until I arrived home and let him know.

Approaching a stop sign, I came to a complete stop. One other car sat at the four-way stop. A red luxury car proceeded across the road.

Exhaling, I closed my eyes and rubbed my neck. Zach would need to give me a massage tonight to get rid of the stress knots that I had.

Opening my eyes, I stared into the darkness. No longer did I sit in my car, headed home after a wonderful girl's night. I was back in the dark, all alone.

Did I just remember what happened on the way home from Emma's house? Or was my mind playing tricks on me?

So many things had crossed my mind since being in isolation. It was hard to decipher what was real and what was make believe. Was I hallucinating?

Something about that memory, though, felt real. I knew I had lived it. The night that I couldn't remember for my life hit me like a shock wave.

What happened after the red car passed? Did someone intercept me at the four-way stop? Did someone intercept me farther down the road? Did they follow me home? Or did they lie in wait, waiting for me to arrive home?

Following me home would make more sense. Fewer people would observe anything occurring at home than if they did anything while on a frequently driven road.

Another noise sounded from above, this time louder.

Raising my knees to my chest, I wrapped my arms around my legs. Rocking back and forth, I anticipated meeting my captor.

A metal lock sounded. Seconds later, a door creaked.

Looking up towards the stairs, I tried to make out any features to see if the person was a man or a woman. All I could make out was a dark figure swallowed in a black hoodie. Even with the door open and the small amount of light that came in, I couldn't make out much.

The person closed the door behind them, placing me in complete darkness. Seconds later, footsteps sounded on the stairs.

As they walked down the stairs, my nerves intensified. My heart beat quickened, pounding in my ears. My hands turned clammy.

Scurrying off the bed, I went to the farthest corner of the cage, farthest away from the door and lowered myself.

I didn't know the reason for their visit. To my knowledge, this was the first time they had made themselves known. Did they come to finish me off? Did they come to provide more torture? So many questions, and I doubted I would receive any answers.

"Who are you?" I blurted.

Keys jingled before they entered a lock. The swift sound of the lock turning forced me farther into the corner. The cold metal bars dug into my back.

"Hello," I called out, my voice coming out weak. It lacked every bit of confidence within me.

Silence. If a pen dropped, anyone within a small radius would be able to hear it.

The door slid open. The door screeched to a halt when it opened all the way. Standing in the doorway was the devil himself.

"Why are you doing this to me?"

From where I sat, the person stood ten feet away. Even though they stood so close, they appeared so far away. Was I shrinking? Was this place much bigger than it was seconds ago?

"Please, let me go."

My pleas fell on deaf ears. Question after statement, they continued to ignore me, as if I wasn't even talking.

I couldn't make out if the person was tall or short, lanky or had a few extra pounds , or if it was a man or a woman. The pitch-black darkness provided me with no details. If they at least gave me the decency of answering, I could guess their gender. Maybe that is what they wanted to conceal. Or perhaps I would know the voice if they said anything. Was it someone I knew?

Would it make a difference if it was a man or woman who held me hostage? If it was a man or woman, did I have a chance of fighting my way out of this hell hole if given the opportunity? I highly doubted it. My chances of fighting anyone right now weren't great. At the right time, I would react. Right now wasn't the time. I lacked every ounce of strength known to man.

Squinting my eyes, I tried my hardest to make anything out, but they concealed their identity well. This person was calculated. They thought of everything.

"What are you going to do with me?"

That was the hardest question to ask. On the one hand, I wanted to know what they planned to do with me. On the other hand, I wasn't sure if that information would be fine for my mental health.

They set a tray and a cup on the bed before they grabbed the empty tray and cup.

Once they walked out of the makeshift cage, I gathered the strength to stand up. Walking towards the opening, they slid the gate back into place before they locked it.

Approaching the door, I inhaled, attempting to catch a feminine or masculine scent. Unfortunately, the only thing I smelled was Irish Spring.

"Please, don't leave me here."

The person just stared at me. They didn't move a muscle. They didn't make a sound.

They turned and walked towards the stairs.

"Can you at least give me some blankets? Something, it's freezing down here."

The person stopped on the third step. They waited for a moment before they turned around and looked at me once more.

I stepped back, unsure if I had set off an unwanted firework in them.

They turned back around and continued up the stairs.

"Please..." I called out, but the door had already been closed and locked.

A lump lodged in my throat. Trying with

everything in me, I tried to swallow it down, but it was no use.

Salty tears streamed down my face. I grabbed a metal bar and pulled on it, hoping it would move, even though I just watched it being locked.

Sliding down to the ground, all my emotions hit me full-force.

I wouldn't see daylight again. Never would I be able to see a sunrise or a sunset with my husband's arm wrapped tight around my waist. Luckily, we had that experience the Monday when we came back home . It felt like years had passed since I last saw Zach.

I wouldn't see outside of this basement again. Breathing fresh air and feeling the grass under my toes seemed like a luxury now. I now cherish all the things I used to take for granted with all my heart.

I wouldn't see my husband again. What I would do to see his beautiful smile right now. My heart ached, knowing he was going through just as much hell as I was going through. The only difference was that he went through hell on the outside, looking for me like a chicken with its head chopped off. I went through hell on the inside, not knowing if I would live for another second, minute, hour, or day.

Crawling to the bed, I pulled myself up on top of it. Eyes squeezed shut, tears continued to fall.

What I would do to have Zach's arms wrapped tight around my waist. Rubbing my hands up and down my cold arms, I remembered the first time Zach took me to his home, our new shared home.

Staring out the passenger window, greenery passed in a blur. We were getting closer and closer to Sacramento, the city that changed my life forever. My heart pounded louder and louder as we approached the exit we would take to get off the freeway.

Fingers intertwined with mine, momentarily distracting me. I pulled my eyes from the window and looked at Zach.

"Are you okay?"

Was I? Both threats to my livelihood were placed behind bars less than fifteen hours ago. That gave me a sense of calm and safety, but that didn't change the outcome of one of their decisions. Even though justice for Candace would come in due time, it would never bring her back.

"I'm okay," I answered.

Zach lifted my hand, tugged his eyes away from the road briefly, and placed his lips on the back of my hand.

"I'm just not sure if I should move in with you…"

"Destiny, we've gone through this already," Zach interrupted me as he placed his attention back on the road. "I refuse to let you move back into that apartment. There are too many memories there and you will never be at peace."

"Yes, I know I can't stay in the apartment, but

I could move back with my parents."

Zach made his transition into the exiting lane for the freeway.

"Do you really want to move states, move back in with your parents, and leave what we have started?"

I opened my mouth to respond, but no words came out. I didn't desire moving back to Florida to live with my parents. I had nothing against the state, but the west coast was my home. The last thing I wanted to do was leave the relationship Zach, and I started. Even though it was the most unorthodox way to start one, I didn't want it to end. I wanted to see where this relationship could go.

"No," I answered truthfully.

"Then, it only makes sense for you to stay with me."

"I don't know." I exhaled as Zach made a turn onto the highway. "I've felt like a burden since you've taken me in."

"I've never viewed you as a burden, and I will never view you as a burden."

As we drove into Sacramento, the familiar feeling of being back in my hometown settled over me. I couldn't imagine leaving there.

"You've done everything for me. You've protected me from the evils in this world, and you've paid my bills. It'll take me years to pay you back on my current salary. I haven't done anything in return except help keep your cabin tidy."

"You've done so much more. More than I could ever explain." Zach gave my hand a squeeze. "I've only seen you as my ray of sunshine. You've shown me not every woman is out to hurt me and tear my soul down. You're my savior."

Zach and his words. Lately, I've been pinching myself more and more, just to prove to myself that I wasn't dreaming Zach into my life. He was real, not a figment of my imagination.

"I promise we can take this relationship as slow as you'd like." Zach flicked his blinker on before he switched lanes. "Relationships are new to me as well. I'm just happy to have you in my life. I don't ever want to make you uncomfortable."

Zach allowed his words to sink in.

"So, what do you say?"

Flicking my eyes over to him, I smiled.

"I will stay…"

Zach whooped and hollered before I could even finish my sentence.

"Only if you allow me to contribute around the house."

"Yeah, yeah." He patted the seat in between us. Scooting over, Zach wrapped his arm around my waist and peppered kisses to my forehead. "In just a few short minutes, you'll get to see your new home."

Five minutes later, Zach turned into a neighborhood I had never visited before. All the lawns were beautifully maintained, no flaw in sight. Even though I had spent most of my life in the city, I hadn't known anyone who lived there. Now, I lived there.

After passing several houses, we made a left-hand turn. We passed a few more houses before Zach pulled into a driveway.

I looked up at the Cape Cod styled house. The house was navy blue with white trimmings.

"Your place is beautiful," I commented once Zach opened the passenger door.

Grabbing his hand, I stepped out.

He placed his hand in the middle of my back and said, "Thank you, but you haven't even seen the inside of our place yet."

Our.

We actually shared a place together, yet I didn't even know what it looked like on the inside. Everything in me told me that the inside looked just as amazing as the outside.

He led me up the cobblestone path as I admired the Verbena de la Mina lining the border of his house.

As he unlocked the door and pushed it open, he said, "I will get you a house key made later today."

A burst of cool air hit me as we walked into the foyer. A gorgeous silver chandelier hung above, and my jaw instantly fell open.

"Oh my," I gasped.

"You haven't seen anything yet," he said as he closed and locked the door.

He walked me into the living room, which was tastefully decorated. Another chandelier hung in the living room, casting the whole room in a magnificent light. There was a tan L-shaped couch and a small, brown coffee table in front of it. Fake plants littered the living room's corners, bringing out an earthly feel.

"You really love your fake plants," I observed.

Zach chuckled. "Yes, I do. I can't kill them, and they look just as amazing as the real thing."

He led me to the kitchen and dining room. The black appliances matched perfectly with the brown cabinets and light-colored marble countertops. In the corner sat a black circular table for four with matching chairs, adorned with a small plant.

"Do you have an obsession with plants?" I asked him as I looked at him over my shoulder.

He wrapped his arms around my waist and kissed my cheek. "I would like to say no, but my house proves otherwise."

"If you don't mind, I would love to bring a little more life into your decor."

"I would absolutely love that."

Zach guided me out of the dining room area and we walked towards the back of the house and down a hall. There were three doors, two on the left-hand side and one on the right-hand side.

He showed me the guest bedroom, which had a queen-sized bed covered with a gray comforter, a chair, a dresser and a nice-sized TV.

"Do you have guests come over often?" I asked.

Zach entwined his fingers with mine. "On the

rare occasion, Jake will stay over if he's had one too many, but that's about it."

"What a wonderful best friend you are," I replied before I gave his hand a squeeze.

Afterwards, he showed me the guest bathroom, which had a shower. The room was adorned in gray decor.

"Now, it's time for you to see your new bedroom."

Zach opened the door, and my mouth dropped in awe.

Sitting in the middle of the room was a king-sized bed adorned with a dark blue comforter. A massive dresser sat across from the bed, which housed a TV. Two end tables sat on each side of the bed, topped with a small fake plant. A chandelier matching the others in the house sat directly above the bed.

"If that bed feels just as comfortable as it looks, I'm going to sleep like a baby tonight."

"Yes, you will." Zach led me to a closed door. "Especially after you soak in here tonight." He opened the door and flicked the light on. On the far right side of the bathroom sat a jacuzzi tub.

Turning around, I looked at Zach. My apartment now seemed like a dump compared to his beautiful home.

"What did I do to deserve this? To deserve you?"

Zach placed his hands on my waist, pulled me forward and kissed my forehead.

"You showed me what love was."

***

Gasping, I pushed myself up to a sitting position. On the verge of a panic attack, I slapped my hands on my forehead, trying to catch my breath.

The darkness was suffocating. All I wanted to do was go back to the home Zach, and I shared.

If I had to spend my last few moments stuck in this place, I'd do it reminiscing the best memories I shared with Zach. The thought of seeing him again kept me sane, even if it was in my dreams.

Chapter Thirteen

Zach

"Do you think you should slow down on the coffee?" Jake asked me once he set the cup on the coffee table.

He sat beside me on the couch.

"No, I'm just getting started."

Grabbing the cup, I took a sip. Jake rubbed his eyes before he cradled his own cup of coffee.

"How long have you been up?"

Did he want a lie or the God's honest truth?

"Only two hours."

Jake scoffed as he looked at the time.

Jake had stayed the night last night. He constantly worried about me, especially when he asked me how I was doing, and I replied, "I'm fine."

Everyone within a thirty-foot radius could tell I wasn't, but I lied anyways. It made things much easier for me because no one expected an explanation after that response.

"Two hours, my ass." He pointed at me with a worrisome look in his eyes. "You have bags under your eyes."

Reaching up, I touched my eyes. They were puffy.

"Okay, fine."

I refocused my attention back to my laptop. I had a bunch of tabs open.

"I've been up for hours, but I'm on to something here."

Jake exhaled before he rubbed his temples with his thumbs.

"Zach, what are you doing? You have to take care of yourself. If you don't, you won't be any good to Destiny if you find her ."

Tugging my eyes away from my laptop screen, I stared at Jake. Time slowed down.

"I meant when," Jake corrected himself.

When was correct? There was no if in the situation, and there never would be. Destiny was out there somewhere, waiting for me to rescue her. I just had to find her.

Refocusing my attention on my laptop, I tapped my fingers as I focused on the information displayed about Melissa.

"All I'm saying is you have to take care of yourself." Jake stopped drinking his coffee. "No one can just survive off coffee. Even Superman has to get a few hours of rest at night."

"Superman has nothing on me when it comes to Destiny."

"Zach."

I looked at Jake.

His eyes pleaded with me.

"Please, just listen to me with an open mind and an open heart."

Ooh, boy.

I didn't expect sappy Jake to make an appearance, but there he was.

"I know you're going to be upset with me but..."

He grabbed my computer off my lap and closed it.

Opening my mouth to object, Jake continued.

"You need to get some rest. I'm not only talking to you as your best friend but as your brother."

"Everyone is counting on me to bring Destiny home," I pointed out.

Once I informed Destiny's parents, her mom and stepdad were ready to book the next flight into town. After talking them off the ledge, I told them that coming right now wouldn't bring Destiny home any faster. It might slow the process down, considering I would be worried about making sure they were okay while here, on top of doing everything I could to find Destiny. Her dad wanted to help me find her as well, but I told him to leave it to me. I wouldn't stop until I brought Destiny home.

Emma and Hannah were both on my case, requesting updates through text multiple times a day. Hannah was more on my case than Emma, simply because Emma's direct contact with me was Jake, and he tried to encourage her not to contact me as much since I was so focused on locating Destiny.

"I understand everyone is counting on you, but it's something even if you get only three or four hours of sleep. You need to rest your eyes and mind for a few hours."

Jake might be right. I hadn't slept more than two hours at a time without waking up to an image of Destiny lying in a ditch. My mind played major tricks, preventing me from getting adequate rest, but Destiny's safety was more important than my rest.

"Okay," I responded after an exasperated exhale.

Jake grabbed my phone off the coffee table and slipped it into his pocket. He pointed towards the bedrooms.

"Go ahead, get some rest."

Placing one heavy foot in front of the other, I made my way to the hallway. Turning to look over my shoulder, Jake waved at me before his phone rang.

Walking down the hall, I was out of Jake's sight. I placed my back against the wall and waited for him to answer his phone. Yes, I had no business snooping, but being on edge with so many crazy thoughts going through my mind made me do crazy things.

"Hey baby, what's up?"

Jake was quiet for a few moments.

"He's okay. He hasn't been resting, so I took his laptop and phone and made him lie down and get some rest."

Silence.

"Yeah, I can leave here in a few. I have no problem taking them to school."

Great. Jake would be out of my hair sooner than expected, so I could get back to my searching. I was onto something. I was headed down the right path in my search.

"Let me go check on Zach, finish my coffee, and I'll be there. I love you, Emma."

Tiptoeing down the hall, I disappeared into my room. Softly closing the door behind me, I jumped into the bed, laid down and covered myself up. It pained me to lay in this bed without Destiny, but I had to do what I had to do until Jake left.

Closing my eyes, I slowed my breathing.

Five minutes later, I heard the doorknob turn.

"Zach," Jake whispered.

I stayed silent, hoping he would think I was asleep.

"Zach," he whispered again.

Footsteps sounded, and I squeezed my eyes tighter.

"I knew you were tired," Jake said as he chuckled.

After I heard the door close, I waited several seconds before I sat up and pushed the blankets off me. I loved Jake with all my heart, but he didn't know what was best for me.

I walked out of the bedroom and made a beeline for the living room. Walking to the window overlooking the front yard, I watched as Jake got into his SUV.

Perfect. I could get back to my research.

My phone rang as I walked over to the couch. I exhaled when I saw Frank's name. What could he possibly want?

"Hello."

"What the hell is going on with you?" he fired off.

Pulling the phone away from my ear, I looked at the phone in disbelief. There was no way this man called me and started yelling at me.

"The real question is, what the hell is wrong with you?" I asked him once I placed the phone back to my ear.

"You should not have gone to the prisons to talk to Trevor and Melissa. That was my job to do."

"It might've been your job, but you are taking too damn long to get information on my wife's disappearance," I emphasized the word job.

"I have to follow protocol. You know this, Zach."

Rolling my eyes, I plopped down on the couch. "Protocol, my ass. There is no protocol when it comes to Destiny."

I had never said anything truer than that statement.

"You've overstepped your boundaries by the visits you've done. You've overstepped your boundaries by not allowing me to do my job. Do you really want to risk losing your job? You know you can't handle Destiny's case."

"I'll risk my life for my wife," I stated firmly. "This job can be replaced. My wife can't be."

I had requested Family Medical Leave the night Destiny disappeared. No way in hell could I go into the office every day and work while my wife was out there, hoping at any second that I would rescue her. I'd spend every moment looking for her.

Frank exhaled. "You've always been stubborn." He paused. "What did Trevor and Melissa say to you?" Frank asked.

"They didn't say too much of anything."

"There is no reason to lie, Zach. We are on the same team here."

I chuckled under my breath. Frank dug at my character, and it pissed me off.

"It's crazy that when I suggested that Trevor and Melissa had something to do with this, you shot that idea down."

"Theory," Frank corrected me.

"Theory," I spat out in a fiery tone. "Since you didn't think that theory was worth going after, I went after it myself. Trevor didn't know anything, and Melissa, she's just the devil in a woman's body."

"What do you mean by that?"

Sitting back on the couch, I closed my eyes, willing my anger not to erupt.

"Melissa implied she knows who kidnapped Destiny."

"Oh damn." Frank exhaled. "Are you sure?"

"Yes, I'm sure."

Opening my laptop, I entered my password and stared at the open tab. This phone call needed to end so I could get back to my research.

"I'm going to go investigate Trevor and Melissa myself. Zach, just stay out of my way. This is my case to solve."

"Yeah, yeah." His words went through one ear and out the other. "Did you get fingerprints off Destiny's phone yet?"

"Nothing yet. You know that it can take up to a month for fingerprints to come back."

Yet, he wanted to get fingerprints off the phone before he even looked into the possibility of Trevor or Melissa being responsible.

"I'll keep you updated with any information I receive, okay?"

After I hung up the phone, I focused on my laptop. When it came to finding out who was closest to Melissa, I had to look at her life in its entirety. She might not know where Destiny was, but she had to know what happened to her.

If I were in Melissa's position, who would I trust the most to handle something I didn't have the capability to do? I'd trust either my current partner or an ex-partner if we left off on good terms.

Melissa made it evident she didn't trust Trevor to do anything right. Trevor convinced me that he had nothing to do with what was happening. Trevor was officially off my suspect list. He was just a man caught up in a situation where his mistress was taken from him, and he felt the need to protect his wife, whom he had betrayed. He was pulled down a rough path by his manipulative wife.

Perhaps Melissa had exes that might've still been in her life. All I had to do was find them online and look further into their lives.

Due to my social media searches, I was able to dig up posts from several years ago. I came across two men that Melissa had dated before Trevor came into the picture. She dated a man named Dominic, and another man named Edgar.

First things first, we would start with Dominic. After searching for Dominic's first and last name, his social media profile appeared first in the search. Clicking on his profile, I exhaled. Dominic was a dead end, leading me down a path that wouldn't result in me finding my wife. According to his profile, he lived in Utah.

The last time he posted was twenty-three hours ago. His arm was wrapped tightly around his wife's shoulder. Three small, elementary school-aged children stood in front of them. They were wearing matching Hawaiian attire with a scenic ocean view. The post stated, 'Hawaii, you were one amazing home for a whole week for my family and me. We can't wait to come back.'

Dominic wasn't in California when Destiny was kidnapped. He was in Hawaii, enjoying its natural beauty and all the wonderful attributes the state had to offer. Also, he seemed more than happy with his family. He didn't seem to be a man to mess with his family for an ex stuck behind prison bars for murder.

Dominic could officially be checked off the suspects' list. Now, onto Melissa's second ex, Edgar.

Edgar was Melissa's second boyfriend. When I searched him up, it was evident she had a thing for men in uniform. Edgar was in the army. Currently, he was stationed in South Korea. From the looks of things, he had been stationed there for a while. He hadn't been in the States in months. He couldn't have possibly kidnapped Destiny.

Cursing under my breath, I crossed Edgar off the suspect list. Damn, I was back at square one with no suspects. There was no one with the ability to lead me where my wife could be.

My whole morning had been wasted on Melissa's exes.

Now, it was time to look into the family.

As my fingers flew across the keys, my

phone rang. Hopefully, that wasn't Frank calling back with his shenanigans.

Tugging my eyes away from the laptop screen, my heart pounded in my ears. Time seemed to slow down. Blocked number stared back at me as it continued to ring.

This might be a call concerning Destiny. This wasn't the first unknown call I had received since Destiny's disappearance. I had received several, but something about this call seemed different. Due to it being quite early in the morning, something was up with this call. I had to answer it.

After clicking into the cell tower triangulation app, I answered the phone and closed my laptop.

"Hello."

"Z-Za-Zach."

My heart sank into the pit of my stomach as I stood up. A sour taste filled my mouth, forcing a scowl onto my face. It was Destiny.

"Destiny," I gasped. I walked towards the front door. "Are you okay? Are you alone? Where are you, baby?"

She let out a horrific cry, shooting a dagger straight through my chest. "I don't know where I'm at, but I'm so scared."

Dropping my keys, they clattered to the floor. I stilled my movements.

The fear in Destiny's voice caused me excruciating pain. There she was, on the phone with me and I couldn't do anything to help her.

Destiny completely skipped over my first two

questions, which alarmed me in more ways than I could explain.

"Who is there with you?"

It was pertinent for Destiny to answer that question. If she had that information, tracking her down would be so much easier. I'd have something, considering I didn't have too much of anything right now.

Destiny paused.

"I-I don't know."

All I had to do was keep talking. All Destiny had to do was keep talking. The longer I kept her on the phone, the better chance I had at tracking her.

"I'm going to find you, I..."

A click rang out, interrupting my spew of words.

Pulling the phone away from my ear, I stared at the ended call.

Damn it. No, no, no. Due to the person calling with the block on their phone, I was unable to call the number back. I yelled out, "Shit."

Running back to the couch, I sat, opened my laptop and went to work.

Destiny was alive. She was alive and well, just scared out of her mind. Hopefully, the

call was long enough to track. If it was the last thing I did, I would find Destiny.

Hearing her voice warmed my heart. Just knowing she was still alive ignited a fire under my ass. I needed to bring her home.

I yearned to hold her in my arms. It had only

been three days since she was last in my arms, and it seemed like an eternity. Her body fit perfectly in mine. She was made especially for me.

I desired to kiss her sweet lips. There was no better way for Destiny to show her affection to me than planting her scrumptious lips on me every day.

I yearned to be in her presence. Without her around, I was a ball of yarn, useless to anyone close to me.

I would give anything to bring Destiny home. Once I had her in my grasp, I'd never let her go.

I've saved her before.

I'd save her again.

Chapter Fourteen

Destiny

Staring into thick blackness, I gasped for air. Pushing myself up to a sitting position, my heartbeat quickened. I needed to get out of there now.

I stumbled off the bed, my legs feeling like noodles. Once I got my footing, I ran towards the door. Attempting to pull it open with all the strength I could muster, I exhaled in anger. The door didn't budge.

How much time had gone by? Had it been three weeks? Had it been a month? Had it only been two days?

It was hard to keep track of time when I was in the dark. Every second, every minute, every hour felt like an eternity. With every second that passed by, I lost myself even more. Would I ever be myself again?

How did my parents feel? Did they even know I was missing? We talked on the phone at least twice a week. If it had been more than a week, I know they'd already called. Going into protective custody two and a half years ago made them so stressed they literally pulled their hair out. During that time, I was under Zach's protection. This time around, I was missing, and I had no idea who held me hostage or where I was located.

How did my friends feel? One second, I was with them having a heartfelt moment. The next second, I woke up in this hell hole after briefly remembering being at the four-way stop. What happened after that four-way stop? Did I ever leave that location? Did I manage to arrive home? Will I ever remember? I sure hoped so. Maybe remembering those moments before I was kidnapped would give me insight into who is responsible for this.

Most importantly, how did my husband feel? I'm glad my kidnapper allowed me to call Zach. Don't get me wrong, I was completely terrified when the basement door creaked. Heavy footsteps came down the stairs, sending me into a frenzy. I didn't know the reason for their visit, and I didn't want to find out. All I knew was that I wanted to live to see another day. I needed to live so I could see my husband again. The love we shared was what kept me going.

When the gate opened, I crouched in the corner with my head tucked into my lap.

When my kidnapper walked into the cage, I lifted my head and stared at the open gate. For a split second, I considered making my escape. Deep down, I knew I didn't have enough strength to make a run for it. Perfect timing was key, but that time wasn't now.

A dark figure hovered over me. Craning my neck up, I opened my mouth to speak, but every thought escaped me when the figure leaned down, hooked their arm through mine and pulled me up off the floor.

"Please, don't hurt me," I pleaded.

A basic, black phone was pulled out of their jacket pocket with a gloved hand. I quickly looked at the date and noticed three days had passed. My heartbeat quickened as they went into the contacts when I saw Zach's name.

If there was any doubt in my mind that this wasn't planned, that doubt immediately left me.

The phone was placed on speaker. The phone rang so many times I feared Zach wouldn't answer, but when his sweet voice called out, "Hello," my heart filled with love.

It had been three days since I last heard his

voice.

"Z-Za-Zach." I called out, my voice raspy.

"Destiny," he gasped. "Are you okay? Are you alone? Where are you, baby?"

A hand tightened its grasp on my arm, and I screamed out in pain. If that squeeze didn't leave a bruise, I'd be surprised.

"I don't know where I'm at, but I'm so scared."

The grip loosened up on my arm, giving me temporary relief. I did exactly what they wanted me to do, whatever that was.

"Who is there with you?"

"I-I don't know," I answered truthfully, flicking my eyes to the monster beside me. Boy, I hated the mask they wore over their face. Hell, if I knew, I would've given that information up as soon as he answered the phone.

"I'm going to find you, I..."

A gloved thumb touched *end call*, sending a dagger straight into my heart. The phone was immediately powered off.

"Why did you do that?" I heard myself yell.

Anger boiled within me as the person unhooked their arm from mine and shoved me with their arm.

Stumbling back, I fell into the cold, hard metal.

The figure walked towards the open gate. Once the door was locked, they lifted their head and stared at me for a moment before they approached the stairs.

I ran over to the gate, and banged on it.

"I'm freezing. Can you bring me blankets?"

They paused briefly on the second step before they continued their way upstairs. Once the door closed and locked, I walked over to my bed and lay down. Tears spilled out of my eyes, wetting my cheeks.

Was I pathetic? How could I reference this hard piece of material as my bed? My bed was back home in the two-bedroom home I shared with Zach. It was a plush king-sized bed, currently adorned with a red comforter. This twin-sized thing couldn't be my bed, yet I was forced to sleep on it.

What was their purpose in calling Zach? What was their purpose in having me talk to Zach, just for them to hang up mid-conversation? I'm glad Zach knew I was still alive. That must've been a relief for him. What royally pissed me off was them ending the phone call mid-sentence. There's no way in hell Zach's mindset was fine right now. Did they want Zach to suffer? Did they want me to suffer? It only made sense that they wanted both of us to suffer.

They gave us a piece of what we wanted, to talk to each other. Yet, they pulled that piece of hope away by ending the call so rapidly. If I knew Zach as well as I thought I did, he went to work on finding the identity behind that phone number. Sadly, he wouldn't find too much from that call. It was obvious to me that it was a burner phone. The calculated thoughts of this person scared me crapless.

How had it only been three days since I was kidnapped? Being down in this basement, freezing my ass off, felt like an eternity I would never, ever escape.

Hearing Zach's voice fueled the part of me that considered giving up. His voice was medicine to my broken spirit because I was on the verge of giving up mentally, physically, and emotionally.

What did I do to deserve this type of torture? What did I do to deserve this type of treatment?

Yes, my kidnapper fed me two meals a day, which consisted of a nasty, dry sandwich with lunch meat I couldn't figure out and water that didn't taste the best. Those meals were essential, nothing close to luxury. They gave me just enough to hydrate and sate my hunger for a little while. They hadn't given me the right amount of food to gain strength, but I hoped the less I bothered them, the better off they'd treat me. Wishful thinking, I was stuck in the pits of a caged, metal hell.

Was it a man or a woman who was there with me? There was nothing masculine or feminine about their scent. Was the person relatively taller than me, or were we the same height? I was too scared to size them for fear of my safety. The person did squeeze my arm pretty well, but I couldn't feel if the force came from a woman or if it came from a man.

There were so many questions I had about this person's identity. They stood beside me, and I still knew nothing about them. I should be ashamed of being a detective's wife. Had I not learned anything since I've been with him?

Rubbing my hands up and down my arms, I closed my eyes tight, willing the tears to cease. I didn't have time to feel bad about myself. Right now, I needed to figure out a plan on how to make my escape. Everything had to be perfect in order for this escape to pan out in my favor. All I had to do was think like my husband.

Wiping my face clear of tears, I allowed a sob to escape. Most newlywed couples probably didn't have issues like Zach and me. Our issues didn't stem from anything we did to betray the other. Our issues stemmed from someone in our world wanting revenge. Revenge, for some, was a sweet, sweet victory.

Fluttering my eyes close, I went to a happy place. A place where Zach's love and presence surrounded me.

"Now, it's only fair for me to make love to you."

I was back in our home, our pleasant tour coming to an end.

Spinning around, I faced Zach. I dragged my finger from Zach's navel to his collarbone.

"Oh really?" I asked.

Zach placed his hands on my waist and pulled me close. He dragged his tongue from my neck, and up to my ear. That move alone had me like putty.

"Yes, really," he answered before he captured my mouth. Once his tongue slipped into my mouth, my knees instantly went weak.

Zach quickly wrapped his arm around my waist and held me up.

"You don't want to give me some time to wash up and settle in?"

Zach hummed as he gave me a playful pinch on my side.

"No, I just want you all to myself."

Zach leaned forward with his lips puckered. Turning my head at the very last second, he kissed my cheek.

He chuckled before he grabbed my chin with his hand and stared into my eyes. His brown eyes mesmerized me to my core. "I want you under me, trembling with pleasure."

It was official. His words, combined with his touch, caused a reaction. My panties were wet, my womanhood oozing with juices. I was almost ready for what he had in store. Almost.

He went for my lips again, and I placed my index finger between them. His eyes widened in shock.

"Are you teasing me right now?"

Wiggling my eyebrows, I responded, "Maybe." My eyes flicked over to the bathroom. "I think I need that soak right now."

Zach placed his lips on my forehead, and I basked in the love and attention he had given me.

"I'll go run your bath."

Zach walked into the bathroom, closed the door after throwing a wink my way, and the water turned on.

I stared at the bed, imagining our first night sleeping together in our home. My new home.

I couldn't believe how my life had changed so drastically. I shared rent with my best friend three months ago in a two-bedroom apartment. Now, I lived in this beautiful two-bedroom, two-bath home with my boyfriend. If things had progressed this quickly, I wondered what else would happen.

Was I ready for this type of commitment? I sure as hell hoped so. I knew I couldn't sleep another night in the apartment I shared with Candace. It was bad enough I had to go there and pack up our things. By the time I left there, my eyes would be red and puffy. As I packed, I knew I would reminisce about all the great times we shared.

Walking over to the bed, I laid down on my back and stared up at the ceiling fan. The comforter was silky and soft on my skin.

"Your bath is ready," Zach said once he opened the door.

Sitting up, I looked over at him, and he smiled.

"Are you already enjoying your new bed?"

"It's so comfortable," I answered as I walked towards him.

"How about we enjoy it together right now?"

"Maybe after my bath."

Gasping, I threw my hand over my heart. Red rose petals led a trail to the bathtub. The bathtub overflowed with vanilla-scented bubbles. On each corner of the bathtub were candles.

"Did you have all of this lying around already?" I asked.

We hadn't been separated since Trevor made his unwanted appearance at Zach's cabin. He wouldn't have had the time to do the shopping.

He slipped his arm around my waist and pulled me close, kissing my temple.

"Did you miss the part where romance and love weren't a part of my equation?"

Smirking, I caressed his arms.

"I might've had my mom do some shopping before we arrived."

Beaming, I placed my hand on his chest.

"Your mom is supportive of us already? She hasn't even met me yet."

He nodded as he replied, "She knows how I feel about you and thought it would be a nice act to do for us."

I couldn't wait for the moment when I'd meet his mom.

"Well, tell your mom that I appreciate everything she's done for us."

Turning around, I grabbed the hem of my shirt and lifted it over my head. Unclasping my bra, it dropped to the floor in a heap. Covering my arm over my breasts, I turned around and winked at Zach.

"Are you coming to join me?"

"No, I need to do a few things around here while you relax."

Slipping out of my pants and panties, I tossed

them onto the heap on the floor. Zach slapped my butt before he helped me into the bathtub.

The bubbles surrounded me as I settled into the warm bath. If I could explain how it felt, it was similar to floating on a cloud.

"How does the temperature feel?" he asked as he pulled his phone out of his pocket.

"Perfect," I answered.

He put his phone on the vanity beside a plush towel. Calming, instrumental music played, setting the mood.

"Relax, and when you're ready to get out, call for me."

"I will."

Zach smiled before he closed the bathroom door.

Looking around, I basked in the bathroom, which I now call my own. It was twice the size of the bathroom in my apartment. I only had a shower in my bathroom, so I hadn't soaked in a bathtub in years. I'd take advantage of all this bath had to offer.

After twenty minutes, the water was still warm, but I feared my fingers would turn into prunes.

"Zach, I'm ready."

He walked through the door, carrying a soft pink bathrobe. He ran his fingers through my hair before he held his hand out and helped me stand.

He dropped down to his knees, eye level with my stomach. He toweled off my body, showing extra attention to my butt and hips.

"You are so beautiful," he commented.

"Thank you."

Zach slipped the bathrobe on, and I exhaled, loving the warmth it held. He kissed me right in between my breasts before he tied it up, sending shivers up my spine.

Zach led me into the bedroom. A trail of red roses led to the bed, where a heart was created in the middle of the bed by red roses. A bottle of champagne sat in the heart.

"What is this?"

I sat on the bed in awe of the amazing man that stood before me.

"A welcome to your new home celebration."

If I hadn't pinched myself a million times already, I would've thought I was dreaming.

He grabbed the flutes off the end table. After he poured our glasses halfway full, he handed me one as he sat beside me.

"I know things aren't perfect in our lives, but ever since you came into my life, you have made it almost perfect."

He grabbed my free hand and squeezed it.

"I can't wait to see what our future holds."

We clinked our glasses before we took a sip. After grabbing his flute, I placed them on the end table.

Stepping in front of him, I untied my robe and allowed it to puddle at my feet.

He wrapped his arms around my waist and pressed his kisses to my stomach before he looked up at me.

He opened his mouth to say something, but I leaned forward and kissed his sweet lips. Our pecks turned into our tongues, creating a symphony of their own.

In one swift movement, we pulled his shirt over his head. His chiseled chest came into view, and I bit my lip, holding back the temptation to kiss his chest a million times.

He grabbed my head and pulled me back to him, our lips crashing together. He palmed my butt, and we lay on the bed, our mouths never separating.

Straddling him, I rubbed my hands up and down his chest.

He moaned, causing a sensation to vibrate within me.

"Do you want me?" I whispered in his ear.

Flicking my tongue out, I licked his earlobe.

"Yes."

"I can't hear you," I responded as I raised myself to my knees.

Rubbing my hand across his crotch area, his penis hardened as a rock.

Perfect.

"I want you."

His voice was raspy, full of passion. Yet, he wasn't loud enough.

Climbing off the bed, I unbuttoned his pants. I helped him pull his pants down, and his penis sprang to life.

"Louder."

"I want you."

He said it louder, but not to my satisfaction.

Pulling his penis through his boxers, I climbed back on top of him and I stroked him.

"Louder."

"I want you," he yelled.

Lust vibrated in his voice. His eyes pierced me.

"Okay," I simply answered before I grabbed his penis and lowered myself on him.

We moaned in unison as my eyes rolled to the back of my head. He filled me up completely.

"Oh my gosh," Zach gasped as I slowly rode him.

I tossed him a wink as I continued my rhythm. Zach loved to lead, but today, it was my time to please him.

"You like that?" I asked as I bounced on him.

"Hell yes," he called out before he bit the corner of his lip.

My breasts swung, and he reached out and squeezed them before he grabbed my hips.

Our bodies moved in sync as pleasure traveled through our bodies.

"Zach, I'm..." I screamed out as Zach stilled his own movements and groaned.

"I love you, Destiny," Zach said after we came off our euphoria high.

"I love you too."

Snapping my eyes open, my body felt hot all over. Loneliness hung in the dark. Pulling my hands from between my legs, I exhaled. Touching myself wouldn't get me anywhere closer to getting home, but I yearned for Zach's touch, his kiss, his aura.

One day, I would feel his touch again. I wouldn't stop fighting until that happened.

Chapter Fifteen

Zach

Chucking the coffee cup I held across the room, it shattered against the front door. The glass broke into a million pieces as liquid fell from the door to the ground, creating a dark puddle.

Balling my hands into fists, I tried with every fiber of my being not to ram my fist through a wall or a door.

Seventy-two hours. Three long, agonizing days had passed, and I still had no information on the phone call.

It turned out the kidnapper made the call from a burner phone. Sadly, it couldn't be tracked since the person purchased the phone with cash, and they were smart enough not to register the number.

I wasted seventy-two freaking hours chasing information that led me nowhere close to finding Destiny.

In the industry, this was common. Being a detective, running into dead ends was a part of the job description. It was rare not to run into dead ends. Dead ends didn't pan well with me when it came to my search for Destiny. I wanted everything to be smooth sailing. Right now, it was the complete opposite.

I've been down and out since I ran into a dead end when it came to my search for Melissa's ex-boyfriends. Running into this dead end with the burner phone didn't make me feel any better. It made me feel worse, like I wasn't doing my job right. Like I was letting Destiny down.

I could never let Destiny down.

After I grabbed a broom and a mop, I worked on cleaning up the mess I made. Thankfully, this morning, I decided to drink out of a cup I bought at the dollar store on a whim instead of Destiny's favorite cup set.

Once I dumped the contents in the trash bin in the kitchen, I washed my hands and dried them with a hand towel.

My phone sounded in my pocket. Wishing

with all my being that it was an unknown number calling, my hopes dwindled when I saw Jake's name on the screen. After declining the call, I walked into the living room. I had nothing against Jake. He had been my rock during this whole ordeal. Even though it had only been six days, it felt like an eternity. I didn't have anything to say to him right now, but I'd return the call later if he didn't call back first.

As soon as I plopped on the couch, red fury flashed in my eyes.

Destiny's kidnapper intentionally called me from a burner phone to stop the trail I originally followed. Maybe the trail I followed led me in the right direction, and they had to do something to divert my attention elsewhere. Obviously, they knew that the call they made with Destiny speaking to me would lead me to attempt to track the phone call, but they were aware it wasn't traceable. With the phone being purchased with cash, that trail came to a nasty halt since I couldn't trace exactly where the call was made.

It all made sense now. How had I been so dumb not to realize this before? This person reminded me almost like an evil genius. Or was the evil genius controlling her minion on the outside, from behind steel bars on the inside?

I had to get back to my research into Melissa's past. I had spent the last seventy-two hours practically chasing my tail. Now, I had to trace almost every detail from Melissa's past.

This time around, I would start my research

into her family. More specifically, her parents. I grabbed my laptop off the coffee table, and I went to work.

Twenty minutes later, I exhaled as I palmed my forehead. My eyes moved across the computer screen, from left to right, at record speed. This was not the information I expected when I started this research.

There was little to no information on Melissa's biological parents. The reason behind the limited information on her biological parents was that she was adopted. Her birth records, along with the information on her biological parents, were sealed as tightly as a drum.

The information on her adopted parents was sealed as well. The only people able to access this information were the adoptees once they turned eighteen or with a court order if fit.

Did I have enough proof to have those records unsealed? There was a big chance I didn't. There was also a small chance I just might. Considering Destiny's kidnapping might've had something to do with the cases I'd worked on over the years, it didn't hurt to try it.

The last time I searched her social media, I only focused on her relationships. Now, I needed to look at the social media account in its entirety.

The very last post she made was on Christmas Day. She and Trevor stood in front of a huge, brightly lit Christmas Tree. Humongous ornaments hung from its branches. Trevor stood behind Melissa with his arms wrapped around her waist, towering over her by a few inches. They wore thick coats, and they smiled sweetly into the camera. The caption said, *Merry Christmas from the Davidson's. We hope you enjoy your holiday just as much as we will enjoy ours.*

It was crazy to think that just a few days after this picture was taken, Melissa went and murdered Trevor's mistress.

Pictures could be deceiving. Little did anyone know when this picture was taken, Trevor was having an affair with Candace for months. No one could've guessed that behind Melissa's smile was hatred towards her husband's mistress, who she plotted and planned to murder for weeks.

Continuing to scroll through her older posts, I came up empty-handed. She didn't post about her siblings or parents.

Just because she did not post about her siblings, did not mean she did not have any. She had parents, and she never posted them or about them. All she cared to post about were her random quotes about relationships and the relationships themselves.

The only thing left to do was put in a request with the courts to have the records unsealed.

After I filled out all the paperwork, I submitted my request and sat back on the couch. I had done everything humanly possible that could be done at this moment. Things were in motion, and I had to give it time to pan out in my favor.

Glancing at the time, I was surprised to see that it was a few minutes after eleven. I closed my eyes as they were aching from the lack of sleep I'd gotten in the past week.

***

Ringing shook me out of my sleep. Rubbing my eyes with my hands, I looked around the living room. Everything seemed to be in place here, except Destiny's absence. My phone rang once more, and I pulled it out of my pocket.

Frank.

What did he want?

Looking at the phone screen, it was just after noon. I had only slept about an hour.

Going against my better judgment, I waited until the very last second before the phone went to voicemail to answer the phone.

"Hello."

"Woah, Zach." Frank chuckled. "Are you sleeping the day away?"

"Ha ha," I said dryly. I wasn't in the mood for jokes. "If only I could sleep for more than two hours at a time."

Frank exhaled sharply. "On to the important things at hand. Melissa is a piece of work."

I sat up, straightening my posture. This conversation would indeed be the highlight of the day simply because I warned Frank, and he didn't listen.

"Hm. I believe I recall telling you that."

"I thought you were exaggerating, but she proved to me that you were spot on."

Rolling my eyes, I asked, "When have I ever exaggerated?"

Frank thought for a moment before he said, "You're right, you don't."

I headed towards the kitchen. My throat was parched, and I needed water.

"What happened?"

"She gave me the runaround, acting very confused as if she didn't know anything I spoke about."

Once I opened my water bottle, I took a few hearty sips.

"What else?"

"She told me to shove my pen up my ass."

I couldn't help but laugh as I shook my head in disgust.

"Long story short, you didn't get any information from her?"

"Nada," he answered.

"What information did you get from Trevor?"

"That he knows nothing about Destiny's disappearance, and I believe him."

Leaning my hip against the counter, I asked, "Do you honestly believe Melissa isn't involved?"

Silence. The phone was so silent I was almost positive he had hung the phone up before he answered.

"I don't know what to believe."

Dropping my head down, I exhaled. I wasn't sure if it was Frank's tactics that bothered me or his inability to realize the facts shoved in his face. His way of handling cases might've always been this way, giving everyone the benefit of the doubt. It just royally irritated me that he acted this way when it was my wife's life on the line.

"Have you gotten any fingerprints off Destiny's phone?" I asked as I walked into the living room and sat.

"We haven't received any updates on the fingerprints from Destiny's phone yet."

"What the hell is taking so long?" I fumed. "Don't they realize this case is important?"

"This case, as well as the hundred other cases that are going on right now. You know protocol…"

If he mentioned protocol one more time.

"… it's a process. I'm hopeful we will have something back on the fingerprints by next week."

Next week?

Destiny couldn't wait another seven days, another one hundred and sixty-eight hours. It was too risky and far too dangerous. The longer we waited, the more the likelihood of never finding her increased. I didn't want to think like this, but it was damn hard when I couldn't even hold Destiny's hand or wrap my arm around her waist and tell her repeatedly how much I loved her.

"Where do you think your investigation will lead now?"

His investigation had absolutely nothing to do with mine.

"I can interview the people we know who saw her in the three days leading up to her disappearance. Can you provide me with that list?"

"I can send that list right over," I said as my

phone alerted me of a call waiting. Jake's name flashed on the screen. "I have a call on the other line that I have to take."

"Send me over that list as soon as possible," Frank reminded me.

"Yeah, yeah, I will."

Before Frank could say goodbye, I switched the call over to Jake.

"Hey, Jake."

"Zach, are you okay? You didn't answer when I called earlier when I had a break, and you hadn't returned my call."

"Yes, I'm okay. I tried to get some rest," I admitted.

"Really? How did that go?"

"Eh, okay." I shrugged, as if Jake could see me. "Frank called and woke me up."

"I'm glad to hear you got some sleep. Did he having any updates concerning Destiny?"

"No, he just told me that my impression of Melissa was valid."

Jake threw out a chuckle. "Ha, that's the least of your worries," he pointed out.

"Tell me about it," I agreed with him.

"Just because he doesn't have any updates does not mean you don't have any updates. Care to share with me?"

"I know for a fact either Melissa's family members or a friend had something to do with Destiny's disappearance. From what I found, Melissa was adopted. The information on her biological parents and her adopted parents are sealed."

"Holy crap. Really? Is there a way for you to have them unsealed?"

"I've put in a request through the courts an hour ago. We just have to wait and see if they will approve or deny."

"I pray they approve the request. We need to get my sister back."

Jake referring to Destiny as his sister excited me. We were brothers from another mother and as soon as he met Destiny, he saw her as a sister.

"Trust me, I'm working my ass off to make it happen."

I've never worked this hard in my entire life. Sleepless, long nights and early, coffee-centered mornings would pay off.

"I know you are. Would you like to come over for dinner? Emma is making her famous chili, and I know it's one of your favorites."

"No, I think I'm going to stay home."

I couldn't fathom going to hang out with Jake and his family without Destiny, even if it was just for dinner. It just didn't feel right. It felt wrong to have joyful moments while Destiny was only God knows where dealing with whoever kidnapped her.

"Are you sure? If you don't want to come here, I can come over there and hang out?"

Jake's offer to be around me showed exactly how much he loved and cared for me. I wasn't any fun to be around, and I didn't want to bring down the next person.

"No, I don't need any company tonight."

Tonight, I might actually sleep for more than two hours at a time... only if my mind wasn't evaded by horrible nightmares of Destiny being tortured and tormented.

"Can I at least bring you over some chili?"

Could I truly say no to Emma's chili? She's made it for years, and every time she has made it, I would have at least two bowls at a time.

"Yes, I would enjoy that."

"I'll bring you some around dinner time."

After Jake and I said our goodbyes, we hung up.

I placed my phone on the end table and chugged the rest of my water. Now, I needed to do something to keep my mind somewhat occupied.

TV.

That should keep me entertained, even if it's only for a while. Turning the TV on, I clicked into my favorite streaming service. I clicked on the first channel that appeared and stared at the TV. Two men sat on opposite ends of a table while they discussed the latest week of baseball games.

When the show cut to a commercial break, I planted all my attention on the dog food they advertised as a dog on screen ran around, chasing a tennis ball. Destiny and I had discussed getting a dog a few months into our marriage. We were undecided on which type of dog we wanted. We were smack dab in the middle of wanting a beagle or a golden retriever.

The next commercial caused my heart to ache. A realtor company spoke about why they should be chosen as my realtor when it came to finding my dream home.

That's what Destiny, and I were in the midst of doing when she was kidnapped. We had gone to tour a house right before the wedding. We had scheduled to tour another house, but she was kidnapped the day before, so we didn't have the chance.

There was nothing wrong with this house we lived in. It was perfect for a starter family, but we needed something bigger. We didn't want to be in a two-bedroom house anymore. We wanted to upgrade to a three-bedroom so we would have space for our pet and possibly a child if we saw fit in the future.

Attending our first open house together was such an amazing experience. I couldn't wait to attend another one with her. I remembered it like it was yesterday.

As I drove, I looked over to the passenger side of my truck. Destiny looked out the passenger window as we passed by all the beautiful greenery that led us to the beautiful mid-century modern-style house we had our eye on.

It was more on the modern side that Destiny had obsessed over since we discussed finding a bigger house. Also, the house was on an extensive piece of land.

We turned right on a paved road. We drove a fourth of a mile before we arrived at the house.

"Oh my gosh, this place is stunning," Destiny gasped.

The house was white with black trimmings. Plenty of windows lined the front of the house, giving it the modern look that Destiny desired.

Parked in the driveway was a silver Mercedes sedan. A woman dressed in a formal, navy-blue dress that stopped right below her knee walked out the front door, wearing black wedges. She held a white purse in her hand and waved as we parked behind her car.

As soon as I placed the truck in park, Destiny stepped out, spun around in a complete circle, and gasped.

"She's beautiful, isn't she?" the realtor asked, motioning to the house.

"Yes, she is." Destiny walked over to the realtor, and she introduced us. "Hi, Barbara, I'm Destiny, and this is my future husband, Zach."

Barbara's eyes widened as she shook Destiny's hand and then shook mine.

"Future husband?" she asked as her eyes bounced back and forth between Destiny and me. "When's the wedding?"

"Saturday," I answered.

She beamed as she motioned for us to follow her up the path to the front door.

"The wedding day is right around the corner, I love it." She motioned to the stone path. "As you see here, you have a beautiful stone pathway that leads right up to the front door…"

As Barbara took us through the expansive

house, she explained all the amazing things it had to offer. The house had high ceilings, nice wood flooring, and grand chandeliers.

"What do you think?" Barbara asked as we walked down the stairs.

We came to a stop at the foot of the stairs.

"I've died and gone to real estate heaven," Destiny exclaimed before she clapped her hands in excitement.

A screeching sound pulled me out of my memory. I looked around in search of the source. Walking into the dining room, I checked the window. A tree branch had rubbed against the window. I made a mental note to do some trimming soon.

I missed the tone of Destiny's voice when she bubbled with excitement. Hell, I missed her voice. I missed when she would walk over to me, wrap her arms around my waist, and whisper into my ear. She could say the craziest, most bizarre thing to me, and it wouldn't even faze me. As long as I could hear her voice, that's all that mattered.

I yearned to make her happy again. I'd already made her happy in more ways than I could ever count, but finding her and rescuing her would not only make her happy, but it would also make her whole again. It would make me whole again.

Fluttering my eyes closed, a tear fell onto my cheek. With all my being, I hoped she was still alive out there somewhere. Anywhere. I'd look for her until the end of time. I'd fight for her until my

Lost in Love

last dying breath.

Chapter Sixteen

Destiny

"I now pronounce you man and wife. Zachary, you may now kiss the bride."

Zach's bright eyes widened. Closing the short distance between us, Zach looped his arm around my waist. He pulled me into his firm chest and grabbed my chin. Our lips met, and an eruption of applause and cheers filled the room.

A smile peeked through the kiss. We pressed our foreheads together before we made eye contact, the first eye contact as husband and wife.

"You're my wife," he said, just loud enough for me to hear him.

"You're my husband."

Turning onto my side, I pulled the blanket over my arms. Snuggling with the blanket, I enjoyed the warmth it provided.

Wait.

My eyes popped open. Thick blackness still surrounded me. I slowly sat up, confused as to what happened. Obviously, I hadn't woken up in some weird, three-dimensional world where I no longer was held against my will. I knew for a fact that I would remember being rescued and taken from such a hell hole. I yearned for that day to come… if it ever would come.

Touching my lips, I exhaled. It seemed as if a second ago, Zach kissed me, but my dream was vivid. How did I dream about our wedding day? This wasn't the first dream I've had since I've been here that actually occurred and wasn't a figment of my imagination. I've had some memories construed slightly in my dreams, but somewhere in the mix, the memory was there.

I bunched the blanket up in my hands, fearing it would disappear if I didn't have a tight grip.

Where did these blankets come from? How long had I been asleep? The blankets had to have been brought in while I slept.

After all the pleading I did with my kidnapper, they finally provided me with one thing I asked from the day I woke up down here. A blanket. Just because they did one small thing for me didn't make me any less upset with them or the situation. They didn't provide me with all the necessities I should've had if they wanted to treat me like a human being. What I was provided with wasn't anything special, though. I wasn't used to this type of treatment. I'd never get used to it, no matter how long I had to suffer through it.

I pleaded with them to let me go, and yet I was still here. That was one plead I knew would continue to fall on deaf ears.

Nevertheless, I was happy with what they gave me. Actually, I'd say grateful. Even though the blanket smelled horribly of mothballs, it did its job of keeping me somewhat warm.

Wrapping the blanket tight around my body, I scooted to the floor. Slowly, I crawled around, patting the floor for food. When my hand bumped into the tray, I sat on my butt and gobbled the food down, swallowing with so much force that the food wouldn't come back up and make an unwanted appearance. Cupping both hands around the cup, I gulped the water down at record speed. They never gave me enough water to quench my thirst. Just enough to keep me alive, wanting more.

For goodness sake, when it was time for me to get out of this place, I would never eat another sandwich again.

I would never complain about the food they served in the cafeteria at school again. The next time I didn't have time to pack my lunch before work, I would happily savor the taste of the flavorless food they served.

Every time I chowed down on the sandwich, I kept in the back of my mind that I needed all the strength I could muster. The only way I would have the strength to fight off my kidnapper when given the chance was by eating all I could and reserving my energy. Given this blanket, that would be much easier to do. Instead of using all the energy I gained from eating to keep myself warm, I would be able to store some energy for when I would need it the most.

Pushing the tray towards the gate, I crawled back over to the bed and I laid down.

I wasn't sure how long I'd been here, but I was almost positive I'd been here more than a week. I started smelling days ago and yearned for a bar of soap, running water, and a wash cloth. I'd never gone a day without taking a shower or a bath. At this rate, when it was time to get out of here, I'd have to scrub my skin raw to smell decent again.

By now, I knew my parents were aware that I'd been kidnapped. I missed them terribly, all three of them. If I knew anything about my mom and stepdad, they probably got on the next flight into town. My dad probably hounded Zach with every last update or detail he received. Even though he recently came back into my life two-and-a-half years ago, I knew he loved me with all his heart. I learned to forgive him for leaving my mother and me years ago, but I didn't fault him for the decision he made. Just as long as he didn't leave me again… or in this case, I would leave him if I didn't get out of here alive. My leaving wouldn't be a result of my decisions. I just knew I had to do everything I could, which wasn't much, to ensure that didn't happen.

I yearned to see my friends again. When Candace passed away, I didn't have a close friend anymore. Yes, there were still friends on my social media that we went to high school with, but I hadn't gotten together with them in years, and we didn't talk daily. We had that type of friendship where we would send a message once or twice a year to check in on each other. The only person I was truly close with was Candace… until Zach brought me around Emma after he moved me into his house.

Once she introduced me to Hannah and we found out that we worked at the same elementary school, we had been inseparable ever since. I loved every second of the friendship I shared with Hannah and Emma. Time and time again, I've repeated to myself that nobody would ever replace Candace, but I knew deep down that Candace wouldn't want me to sulk around for the rest of my life. She would want me to have close, wonderful friends. The friendship Candace and I shared would never be replaced by anyone. Undoubtedly, we were placed into each other's lives for a reason. My friendship with Hannah and Emma came pretty close to what Candace and I had.

I missed my students dearly. When I was taken into protective custody, I spent months away from them. They allowed another woman to take over my current class, and when they went to second grade, I had the opportunity to have some of them as my students again. It pained me that they would most likely finish the school year without me. Why did this happen to me?

Zach.

No matter how hard I tried not to think about him, he was always on my mind. Not a second went by without him invading my thoughts. Sorrow flooded my veins.

Wrapping my arms around my shoulders, I squeezed my eyes tight. I felt like that woman who ran into the police station two-and-a-half years ago, numb and lonely. I still remember the night he woke me up from the first nightmare I experienced after Candace's death.

Candace. She looked beautiful. With her flawless makeup, she smiled brightly, no imperfection that could be seen for miles.

A gut-wrenching scream escaped her mouth. Her smile disintegrated. We looked at the gunshot wound at the same time before she looked at me. Her eyes were full of pain before she dropped to the ground.

A scream escaped my mouth as a strong force grabbed my arms and held them down by my side.

I kicked, screamed, and clawed with all my

might. They already hurt Candace. They couldn't hurt me as well.

I had to find out who hurt Candace. I was the only witness... to my knowledge.

Right when the murderer's face nearly came into view, everything faded away.

"Destiny."

Who called me? Where did the voice come from? Where was I? Was I dead or alive?

"Open your eyes."

I obliged. I stared into a pair of eyes that were now familiar to me. Zach's eyes were beautiful, so soft and loving.

Snapping my eyes open, I pulled myself out of that dark place. A tear slid down my cheek, and I had no desire to wipe it away.

This person kidnapped me for a reason. They also kept me alive for a reason. The real question to ask was why they kept me alive? There had to be some type of vendetta they held against me or possibly my husband.

There were pros and cons to having a husband in law enforcement. More often than not, the pros outweighed the cons. One big con was people's hatred for my husband, even after several years. It could be the person he put away or one of their friends or family.

If there wasn't a reason behind my kidnapping except for a sick fetish, I'd already be buried in a shallow grave in the middle of nowhere.

All I knew, my heart ached for Zach. At this

rate, I'm almost positive I'd die of a broken heart before dying at the hands of my kidnapper. I just hoped Zach would get the closure he so desperately deserved if I did.

As I fluttered my eyes closed, the sound of a lock sounded. My eyes shot open, my heart pounding in my chest. The pounding was loud. I could hear it in my ears.

I sat up and looked towards the stairs. It seemed like forever before the door creaked open. A hooded figure stood in the door frame. The lights flickered on, and I threw my hands over my eyes. The lights buzzed for a few moments before the silence took over. The silence was eerily loud. The light was blinding, and it hurt my eyes. It had been too long since I'd seen light. Boy, I missed it.

What was so special about today? Why was today, of all days, the right day to turn on the lights? Were they planning to do something with me today? Right now?

Heavy footsteps sounded. Creating a peephole through my hands, the hooded figure was dressed in all black. Their face had a black cover over their face, concealing their identity.

As they stepped closer, they didn't appear as bulky as they had previously appeared the last time I had seen them. Granted, it was pitch black when I saw them last. Was this the same person? Was this a different person? Was there more than one person behind my kidnapping?

Only several feet from me, a floral scent

wafted towards me. I'd smelled that scent before… but from where?

When I blinked, I was behind the wheel of my car. I sat at the stop sign and watched the red car pass.

One of my favorite pop songs came on, and I tapped my fingers against the wheel to the beat after I turned the volume up. Then, I proceeded straight down the road.

The drive from Emma's house to our house was only a fifteen-minute drive. I'd be there in no time.

How was Zach's night going? I bet he and Jake were having a wonderful night. I knew they were at the bar, but I wondered what they did tonight. Were they watching one of the games that played on TV tonight? Were they playing darts or better yet, pool? Or were they just hanging out, catching up with each other? Wedding planning had been so hectic they hadn't really had the chance to sit down and just enjoy each other's company. I'm glad they had the time to do it tonight.

Placing my blinker on, I turned onto our street. Our house was halfway up the street, and I giggled when I noticed Zach hadn't left the porch light on.

Zach and his precautions. He must've been so ecstatic to hang out with Jake he ran out of the house without thinking about turning the light on.

After I parked in the driveway, I killed the ignition. Grabbing my purse, I pulled my phone out.

As I walked up the sidewalk, I unlocked my phone and went to Zach's name.

Right when I went to type my message, an arm wrapped around my shoulders. Glancing down in horror, I noticed the arm was covered by a black sleeve. A floral scent wafted into my nose.

Opening my mouth to scream, I didn't have the chance before my screech was muffled by a white cloth.

Trying with all my might, I tried to wiggle their arm from around my shoulder, but everything went black.

Snapping my eyes open, I uncovered my eyes. Using my hands and feet, I crab-walked away from my kidnapper. It was crazy how a scent could bring my memory back.

The other times they came in here, they made sure not to have a feminine or masculine scent.

The floral scent was the same as the night I was kidnapped. This had to be the same person that kidnapped me. Perhaps it was only one kidnapper.

The kidnapper stood five feet from me. Craning my neck up, I looked at the person before me. They didn't seem as big as they previously had. They didn't seem as intimidating, yet I cowered in the corner.

They lifted their gloved hand and grabbed one side of the face mask. In one swift motion, they removed the face mask and removed the hood from their head.

Gasping, I threw a hand over my mouth. I've seen this person before. What the hell?

Chapter Seventeen

Zach

Rain dropped continuously onto the windshield, the pitter-patter almost therapeutic. It rained hard enough for the two-story craftsman-style house in front of me to look blurry but not hard enough for me to stay in the truck any longer.

Killing the ignition, the windshield wipers stopped mid-swipe.

Stepping out into the rain, I shut the driver's door before shielding my eyes and jogging up the sidewalk.

Right as I formed my fist to knock on the door, it swung open.

Jake looked at me, shaking his head in disbelief.

"I know you were not going to knock on this door like you're a guest, and this is not considered your second home."

Yeah, what was I thinking?

Jake pulled me into a hug and he patted me on the back.

"I'm sorry. I guess I'm losing it," I admitted.

That's how I felt inside. Like a piece of me was missing, and I wouldn't feel whole again until I got that piece back. Destiny was that missing piece. Once she came back, I'd feel whole again. I probably won't let her out of my sight for days. Or weeks if she would allow it, but knowing her, she'd want to return to work as soon as possible because just as much as she missed me, she missed her students.

Jake closed the door behind me as I kicked off my shoes. Fresh ground coffee filled my nose, causing my mouth to water.

"You're going through hell. I'll forgive you this time."

Walking into the living room, I glanced at the TV on the news channel. The last thing on my mind was the latest and greatest current events or the horrible things they preferred to highlight for most of the newscast.

I plopped down in the La-Z-Boy chair. Jake

sat on the couch to the left of me.

Almost as if he read my mind, he grabbed the remote and switched the channel to sports, where men sat around a table and talked about the recent games and their highlights.

"Thank you for inviting me over."

Jake scoffed. "Hell, it only took a million and one invites to get your ass over here. I truly understood how hurt you were when you weren't up to coming over for Emma's chili."

I gave Jake a pointed look.

"Thank you for finally taking me up on the offer."

"I had to get out of the house," I admitted.

I'd spent so much time at home doing my investigation that it felt odd not doing it. The only thing I could see doing there was sleep. That's the last thing I wanted to do right now, though. Resting more than two or three hours at a time was difficult when I wasn't sure if Destiny was getting proper rest.

I tried going to some parks in the area to clear my mind, but all I saw were loving families, either having a picnic or participating in fun activities. Those sights were not great for my mental health, especially when I saw a couple holding hands and laughing in each other's faces as to what the other said while they walked around.

The last place I wanted to go was to work. Actually, going to work was off-limits. I couldn't focus on my job when Destiny was all I could think about. How could I focus on my work when my wife was out there somewhere, in need of my assistance? I hoped like hell she would be fine after this ordeal. Physically, mentally, and emotionally.

I extended my Family Medical Leave since I originally requested two weeks off. I would not go back to work until I could wrap my arms around Destiny's body, kiss her sweet, sweet lips for an eternity, and make sure she was okay.

The only other place I would feel content was being at Meg's Coffee Shop, but being there would only remind me of Destiny. Even though we would only meet up once a week before work, that was a constant in our lives that I missed. I yearned for another morning coffee date before parting ways to go to our jobs.

"I can't even imagine what you're going through," he said.

"Trust me, you never want to know," I answered.

I wouldn't wish this feeling on my worst enemy. It was mental torture.

Having my heart broken into a million pieces was horrible. Nothing could fix it. Nothing could make it whole again… except Destiny coming home. Destiny was the only medicine that would make me feel better. Destiny was the glue that would put the pieces of my broken heart back together.

"Would you like a cup of coffee?"

"I thought you'd never ask," I replied.

Jake stood before he pointed at me.

"Creamer or black?"

"Surprise me."

Jake walked out of the living room. I pulled my phone out to check for any updates, even though my notification volume was turned up. Disappointment washed over me as I put my phone back into my pocket.

Jake walked in, carrying two cups of coffee. He sat the cups on the coffee table before he sat down. Steam swirled from both cups. This was a fresh cup for sure.

"Have you received any updates on the adoption records?"

"No," I answered, getting choked up. I tried to swallow with all my might, but a lump of sorrow lodged in my throat, and it was there to stay.

Sensing my emotions, Jake stood. He motioned for me to stand, and he grabbed me into a bear hug.

A cry escaped my mouth as Jake patted my back. No words were exchanged during our hug, and I was fine with that. Right now, I just needed to cry. I needed to get my emotions out. What better person could I do that with? My best friend, someone I viewed as a brother from a young age.

After a few minutes, Jake and I separated before we sat in our respective seats.

I took a tentative sip of my coffee before he handed me a tissue from the tissue box next to him on the end table.

Wiping away my tears, I balled the tissue in my hand. I knew I wasn't done crying, and I'd need it sooner rather than later.

It had been four days since I requested the adoption records. It was the longest ninety-six hours I've ever experienced.

"How long does it take for the courts to decide if they'll unseal the records?"

Shrugging, I responded, "There is no estimated time. It could be as quick as a week or as long as five or six months."

Jake widened his eyes after he sipped his coffee and placed it back on the table. "Well, we definitely don't want the latter."

"If it were to take that long…"

"I know, I know," Jake finished off for me.

I took another sip of my coffee before I sat it down.

"I'm hoping the judge will see my side of things and have them unsealed as soon as possible."

"What's the likelihood of that?"

"It's a toss-up, but I'm going to hold on to faith."

That's all I could do. With Destiny missing over two weeks, the chances of survival were low under normal circumstances. Deep down, I knew she was still alive. I could feel it within me that Destiny was still out there. I felt so connected with her. I would have known if something had happened to her. I would sense it.

Also, something tells me that this attack was personal. The phone call they made to me with Destiny on the line was a statement. It seemed like they wanted me to suffer, almost in the same way they were suffering. Yet, I had no idea who this person was and what they wanted. Or better yet, the reason behind their actions.

I knew they'd never reveal their identity to me. That would be a dumb move, and this person didn't seem close to being dumb. They knew I'd instantly have a location to go off on finding Destiny if I had that information .

"That's all you can do," Jake responded. "Have you heard any updates on the fingerprints? Were there any other prints on them besides Destiny's?"

Shaking my head, I replied, "The phone is still being processed for fingerprints."

Jake gasped before slapping his leg with his hand. "What the hell is taking so long? It's been two weeks. It shouldn't take this long to get information back, especially when victims are in serious danger."

If only kidnapped victims in this type of situation could be placed in front of other cases.

"Have we at least been able to pull her phone records?"

Grabbing my coffee, I cradled it before taking a sip.

"Yes, we have those, but like I assumed, nothing in there could lead us to a suspect. She's only been in contact with our family, Emma and Hannah."

Jake cursed under his breath.

"Well, that's not much help."

"I know it's a personal attack. Destiny would've been at the bottom of a ditch if it wasn't. The kidnapper wouldn't have made that call if they were planning to kill her."

Jake shook his head in disgust before leaning forward and resting his elbows on his thighs.

"Man, the thoughts that go through your mind constantly are insane. I feel for you, brother. How do you sleep?"

"With one eye open, in small increments."

The honesty rolled off my tongue so effortlessly.

Silence settled over us as we sipped our coffees. The occasional sip would sound until Jake asked another question.

"Were there any cameras in your neighborhood? Maybe someone's camera caught an unfamiliar car leaving in a hurry?"

I scoffed disgustingly.

"You'll never believe it, but no one, and I mean absolutely no one in the area, has a camera."

"Of all the people, I thought you would have a camera." Jake pointed at me. "Especially after everything she's been through."

"We planned on getting a camera at our new home. I had suggested we install one at our current house, but Destiny didn't think it was necessary since we were planning to move."

Jake gave me a pointed look.

"Destiny's an elementary school teacher.

You're the detective here."

I blew air out of my cheeks. Defeat settled over me. If only I had installed those cameras around the house. I would've known who had done this immediately after it happened.

It was horrible how little I knew about my wife's case. Legally, I wasn't allowed to work on it, but damn. Why was that a rule? It just didn't seem right. I was allowed to work hard for someone else's loved one, but not mine? It made no sense.

"I can just feel it." I exhaled as I got comfortable. "I know Melissa's responsible."

"Only time will tell," Jake answered.

"I hope not too much time," I quickly responded. I wasn't sure how much longer I could go without Destiny and stay sane.

If only I could grab Destiny's chin, stare into her beautiful brown eyes, and kiss her sweet, tender lips after telling her I loved her. I had only told her a million times.

Telling Destiny I loved her for the first time was one of the best days of my life. It easily came in third place after the day I proposed to her and married her.

"I haven't felt this way for anyone. Ever." Honesty rolled off my tongue, and nothing in me wanted it to stop.

"What are you trying to say?" she asked.

It's evident she wanted to make sure what she thought was what I would say. I couldn't hold my feelings in anymore.

"I love you, Destiny. I love everything about you, and I don't ever want to see you sad. I hate seeing you go through these emotions every time there's an update. I just want this case to be solved to help you heal. I know it will take some time for you to heal, but I'm willing to put in the time and effort to help you do just that. You've made me want to become a better person. You've made me want to love again. I never thought the day would come when I would say that I love someone again, but I love you, Destiny. I love you so damn much."

My lips crashed onto hers before she could completely process what I said. I had just told her I loved her. I hoped she felt the same way about me.

"I love you too," she said in between kisses, solidifying that we shared the same feelings.

"… Zach."

Tugging my eyes away from the fake plant across the room, I looked at Jake. My vision was blurry, I blinked, and a tear slid down my face.

Jake handed me another tissue, and I exhaled. I placed my coffee down and wiped my tears.

I didn't bawl my eyes out in front of anyone. Since I had turned twelve, I stopped crying in front of my mom. I had to be the man of the household, and I always thought I wasn't manly enough or masculine if I cried. Or if I allowed anyone to see me cry because I had spent plenty of nights crying my eyes out with my covers pulled tight over my head.

I learned that crying was okay once I spent time with Jake and his father. He taught me the true meaning of being a man.

The only person I cried with now was Destiny and Jake.

"Come here," Jake called out.

Jake and I stood, and he grabbed me into another bear hug.

"She's going to be all right."

I hoped he was right. If she wasn't all right, I would never be all right again.

Chapter Eighteen

Zach

A woman with two small children walked by, temporarily grabbing my attention.

"I don't know anything yet, Mom," I replied, trying to focus on the mass of words that spewed from her mouth at rapid speed.

I sat on the bench directly outside of Meg's Coffee Shop. The sun beamed from above and sweat formed on my forehead.

For the last five minutes, Mom had been

interrogating me to the ends of the earth about updates on Destiny.

"... I need my daughter-in-law back."

"I know, I know." I drained the rest of my coffee before I placed the cup on the seat beside me. "We should hear an update any second now," I reassured her.

Who would reassure me?

I only gave reassurance and didn't receive anything back   from anyone else besides Jake. Of everyone involved, I need the reassurance the most. It was my soulmate that had been kidnapped and held against her will. Frank wasn't proving that either.

"You've said that for the last four days," Mom pointed out.

Exhaling, I stood, grabbed my cup, and threw it into the trash.

"I'll keep you updated, Mom."

An elderly couple approached the door's entrance as I turned away from the trash can, and I opened the door and held it open for them.

They mouthed "thank you" when they saw the phone pressed against my face.

"I love you."

"I love you, too," I responded before I hung the phone up and walked to my truck.

It was a bright day with no clouds that could be seen. It would be a beautiful day if Destiny and I were on our way to our jobs. Yet, I was about to leave Meg's Coffee Shop, and Destiny was nowhere to be found.

After I hopped into my truck, I slammed the door shut and started it up. The truck roared to life, and I boasted the air conditioning to the max before I placed my head in my hands.

Everyone depended on me to find Destiny. Hell, I depended upon myself to find her. Nothing that Frank had done thus far had gotten us any closer to whom kidnapped Destiny.

Who could I depend on? I couldn't depend on Frank. He and I weren't on the same page regarding Destiny's case.

I knew for a fact who was the mastermind behind the whole kidnapping. He thought it could be anyone from my past of locking people up for the crimes they committed.

In reality, it could've been, but Melissa's cockiness and deceit told me everything I needed to know.

Melissa wanted me to suffer just as much as she suffered. With Destiny being out there, possibly in pain, I suffered greatly. She got her wish, but in the end, I hoped that, with all my being, I'd be able to bring Destiny to safety.

In the end, I thought it best not to contact Frank. If he contacted me, I'd answer and receive any information he gathered. Still, I knew his searches wouldn't lead to Destiny.

Over the years of working with him, I'd never complained about how he handled his cases. I always thought he was a wonderful detective, a very close second to me. That was before he had to handle the case of my loved one.

I wasn't saying he wasn't a wonderful detective. I still thought he was great. No one could deny that he placed his heart and soul into his work. He worked his ass off, and I couldn't fault him for that. I could fault him for not listening to whom I thought was the suspect.

Melissa was the mastermind. I just had to find who her puppet was... and fast. Time was dwindling down, and if I didn't have some type of resolution soon, I'd go crazy.

Throwing my truck in reverse, I checked my surroundings before I backed out of the parking space and exited the parking lot behind a black SUV.

I wanted to punch myself three days ago when I realized I hadn't even thought about pulling phone calls from the prison. When I first visited, my main concern was getting Melissa to talk. The only thing she left me with when I left the prison was a horrid taste in my mouth. That taste has yet to leave me.

Having phone calls and visitor logs subpoenaed was the farthest thing from my mind when visiting the prisons. Still, I immediately got to work on the paperwork I had to submit to get things rolling.

If Melissa made phone calls, I could subpoena those records and see what had been discussed over various phone calls over a specific timeframe.

If Melissa had visitors, I needed to know who visited, how often they visited, and how long their visits lasted. All this information would mostly lead me down to the person responsible for Destiny's kidnapping.

Some people were smart enough not to discuss anything drastic over the phone. If they dared to talk over the phone, they would use code that they assumed us law enforcement personas weren't aware of. We had an entire dictionary of slang words that meant different things.

Or, they'd have their accomplice come to the prison, and they would talk in person. A guard generally supervised the duration of the visit, but there were ways for everyone to break the rules.

The phone records and the visitor's log for Trevor were sent over immediately. He had proven to me beyond measure that he had no dealings with Melissa, his family, or friends.

The last time he received a visitor was three months into his sentence. His friend Chad paid him a visit. He visited for all of ten minutes, and he had yet to receive any more visitors.

After having done research, I came to the conclusion that there were absolutely no ties between Chad and Melissa. They hadn't been in contact before she went to prison, and they hadn't had any since they closed the metal doors in her face.

The last time he received a call was over a year ago. Listening to that short call, I knew Trevor had told me the truth about not having anyone in his corner.

Melissa's records would take some time to

gather. She had many visitors and phone calls over the last two years. Once I received that information, it would take me some time to sort through it all. I've already mastered surviving off three hours of sleep.

I'd be able to get a great night of sleep once Destiny was back in my arms. Until then, three hours and a load of caffeine would be my savior.

Ten minutes into my drive, my phone rang through the speakers. Glancing at the touchscreen, an unfamiliar phone number appeared.

Clicking the answer button, I called out, "Hello."

"Hello, this is Gina with the county clerk."

All sound ceased to exist. Everything around me moved in slow motion.

The call I had waited for, long, agonizing days, finally came.

"Is this Detective Miller?" she asked, breaking me out of my trance.

"Yes, it is," I answered once I found my voice.

Squeezing the steering wheel tight, my hands turned ash white.

"We have records ready for you to pick up."

That's exactly what I needed to hear.

"I'll be right there."

Ending the call, I threw my blinker on and maneuvered lanes. Once able, I did a U-turn and headed for the clerk's office.

Finally, I received the call that could possibly point me in the direction of who might be responsible for Destiny's disappearance. If I was lucky, it would only be a short few hours until I found my wife.

Putting the pedal to the metal, I arrived at the clerk's office at record speed. Throwing my truck into park, right in front of the building, I flashed my badge at the security guard before he could even open his mouth. He silently nodded and motioned for me to continue my merry way.

Being a detective had its perks, especially when it came to long lines at the clerk's office. I walked past a room full of patrons, and the next available clerk greeted me and went to get the paperwork.

Not even two minutes passed before she came back to the counter. Confidential was stamped in red on the front of the manilla folder.

Once I signed for the paperwork, I made a beeline for the exit.

Should I wait until I arrive home to open the folder? Could I even wait that long? Should I open it right here in front of the clerk's office?

The suspense of not knowing until I arrived home would eat me alive. Once my truck roared to life, I found an empty space in the parking lot.

Staring at the folder, a multitude of thoughts went through my mind. The judge might've approved of my receiving the records, but that didn't mean there was any information inside the folder that would assist me. For all I knew, it could say Melissa's family was well across the country, and I'd be right back at ground zero.

Being at ground zero sucked ass.

Ripping the folder open, I crossed my fingers, toes, and anything else that could be crossed.

Grabbing the thick stacks of papers, my eyes scanned over the information before I stopped at the information I needed.

Melissa's birth parents had three children, two girls and a boy. They were within a three-year age range.

Their parents gave them up for adoption when they were under the age of six. Their birth parent's names were Bailey Hicks and Landon Nickels. No reason was disclosed for the voluntary relinquishment.

They were adopted together by a local family named Richard and Becky Armstrong. They were shy of being a year in foster care by a few weeks.

Grabbing a pen and sticky note from my glove box, I scribbled their parents' names. I'd do a thorough investigation into them once I arrived home.

Her siblings were named Michael and Melinda. Their parents must've had a thing for M names.

Jotting down their names, I placed the file in the passenger seat and dialed Jake's phone number.

"Hey, it's Jake," he called out once he answered on the second ring.

Backing out of the parking space, I replied, "I just picked up the adoption records."

"They're unsealed? What did you find out?

Do you know where Destiny is? When can we go bust that ass? I'm..."

"Wait, wait, wait," I interrupted Jake's spew of words. If I didn't interrupt, he would have gone on for minutes. He didn't play about Destiny.

"What?"

I pulled out of the clerk's office and headed for the highway.

"You won't let me get one word in."

"I'm sorry. I'm just so excited to get some positive information. Anything I can relay to Emma that'll give her some hope would be helpful."

Not only were my mother and my in-laws on my ass 24/7, Emma and Hannah were on me as well. Well, Emma more so than Hannah. Hannah was surrounded by children who needed her full attention all day, so she could only reach out before work, during lunch, and after work. Emma made and sold jewelry part-time for herself. So, she had all the time in the world to reach out to Jake so he could reach out to me for any updates. Honestly, it made no sense why she didn't reach out to me herself.

"At a glance, I could see who adopted her and her siblings..."

"So, she does have siblings," Jake interrupted me once more.

Shaking my head as I drove, I silently chuckled under my breath. His passion to want to know as much information as soon as possible rubbed me perfectly.

"Do you know if they're local? Do you know if her adopted parents are local?"

"I don't, but I'm hoping I'll have all of that information in about two or three hours," I answered as I drove through a yellow light.

"Please, keep me updated. I want to know as soon as you know something."

"I'll call you as soon as I find it out."

After saying goodbye to Jake, I focused on the road. Right as I was about to pull into my neighborhood, I received another call.

"Hello."

"Yes, is this Detective Miller?"

Squeezing the steering wheel, excitement bubbled within. Was it possible for me to get everything I needed to locate Destiny?

"The phone records and visitors log you've requested are ready for pickup."

Drumming my fingers on the steering wheel, I asked, "Is there any way for you to scan that over to me? I'm not in the area, but I need that paperwork as soon as possible."

"Of course. Just provide me with your email address, and I'll send the files secure."

After I rattled off my email address, I hung up the phone. Arriving home in record time, I pulled into the driveway.

As soon as I threw my truck in park, I grabbed the folder and made a beeline for the front door.

I walked through the living room in search of my laptop.

Where did I leave it?

Walking into the bedroom, I saw it on my side of the bed. For the past few days, I'd slept on her side. I tried absolutely everything in my power to feel close to Destiny. It helped for maybe ten minutes, and then I felt even worse afterward.

Tossing the manilla folder onto the bed, I turned on my computer. I had tons of people to investigate.

First things first, I had to start with Melissa's birth parents. Either they weren't married when they gave them up for adoption, or their mother kept her maiden name. I went to work with my search, my eyes scanning the screen rapidly.

Their parents never married. They decided to give them up weeks before they were sent to prison for an aggravated robbery they had committed. Landon received seven years for his part in the crime, and Bailey received five years. I respected them for giving their children up instead of allowing them to be removed forcefully.

After searching for their social media accounts, I came to the conclusion that they had nothing to do with Destiny's disappearance. Once they were released from prison, Bailey went to live in Nebraska, and Landon went to live in Kentucky.

Now that her birth parents were crossed off the list, it was time to focus on her adoptive parents. Typing their names into my search, my heart sunk into my chest. Her adoptive parents passed away in a car accident five years ago. They were involved in a head-on collision with a drunk driver. Boy, I couldn't believe I was going to say this, but I had some sympathy for Melissa. Maybe that was the reason she was bitter. She had been through a lot and she probably didn't know how to deal with her the pain.

Last, but surely not least, it was time to check on her siblings. Since her adoptive parents were no longer on my suspect list, I only had two more people to check.

Finding her brother's social media accounts was quick. Oddly enough, she wasn't friends with him on any of her social media accounts. Turns out, her brother lived in Oregon, more than six hours away. As I scrolled through his page, it became clear how her brother had absolutely nothing to do with Destiny's disappearance. He, himself, was a police officer. He had a wife and a young son. I couldn't see him risking everything he worked for to help his sister commit a crime.

Inputting Melinda's name into my search, my mouth dropped open when her picture popped up.

Grabbing my phone, I dialed Jake's number.

"Tell me you found something good," he said when he answered on the first ring.

"I've seen this person before."

Chapter Nineteen

Destiny

My mouth went dry. Snapping my mouth shut, I rubbed my eyes, hoping my vision wouldn't deceive me.

When I looked at the person before me again, I was dumbfounded.

"H-h-how did you escape?"

A devilish smirk touched her lips before she ran her fingers through her blonde hair.

"I didn't escape from anywhere," she

answered.

Wait. I swore I saw Melissa handcuffed and escorted out of the courtroom. I remembered it like it happened yesterday.

"Is this some type of joke?" I asked as I looked around the cage.

Was I hallucinating? I had to be if I thought Melissa stood before me when I knew for a fact that she was trapped behind metal bars.

"Trust me," she took another step closer to me. "This is no joking matter."

Pushing myself to a standing position, I prepared myself for whatever would happen. I couldn't be a sitting duck when and if I were attacked. I didn't feel like myself. I didn't feel like I had enough strength to defend myself, but I'd do everything in my damn power to do so. Considering she's tried to kill me before, I wouldn't put it past her to try again. This time around, I might not be so lucky. I didn't have the woods to run and disappear into. I was stuck in the biggest way possible.

"Melissa..." I whispered.

I didn't know what to say to her, but I had to attempt to reason with her. Besides, she didn't leave me alive this long for no reason. If she wanted me dead, she would've killed me instead of kidnapping me and bringing me to this horrible place. Unless... she wanted me to suffer before ending my life.

"No, no." She shook her index finger at me before walking back and forth in front of me.

Glancing over her shoulder, I looked at the gate she left unlocked. She stopped walking and looked at me. Looking over her shoulder, she looked in the direction of the gate.

"Let me lock that before you get any funny ideas."

Watching her lock the door, I looked around my area for anything that I could grab and hit her over the head with. Considering this was the first time I could see this place in the light, I was disgusted with how filthy this place appeared, but there was nothing for me to use. Figures, but I had to make sure.

"I know what you're thinking, but I will ease your mind." She shrugged her shoulders as she turned around. "Even if it's just a smidge."

Ease my mind? A smidge? She was even more insane than I originally assumed.

"I'm not Melissa."

My heart dropped into the pits of my stomach. If this wasn't Melissa, did that mean…

"I'm Melinda, Melissa's twin sister."

My heartbeat quickened as I stared at the person before me. I had no knowledge that Melissa had a twin. Did anyone else in this area, besides their family know this? If so, it would've been nice to have been made aware.

Considering the circumstances.

"How? What? What in the hell is going on?"

Melinda went into her hoodie pocket and pulled out a kitchen knife. The edges appeared sharp, glistening in the light.

Placing my hands out in front of me, I gave pleading eyes.

"Chill out with that."

She rolled her eyes.

"I'm not going to hurt you... yet. Things still need to be handled."

Yet?

Gulping with all my might, I tried to swallow the lump in my throat, but it wouldn't dislodge. The yet provided some relief, but the relief immediately disappeared since I didn't know the time frame she referred to. Was the yet in five minutes or in a few days? The more I listened to her, the more I knew I'd never see the outside again.

"Going back to your question of how Melissa and I are twins."

Did she really think I needed a breakdown of what I learned in middle school?

"Our birth parents did the do. One fertilized egg split into two and, surprise, identical twins."

Melinda shook her hands excitedly, making sure to have a tight grip on the knife in her hands.

Wait. Birth parents? Nobody referred to their birth parents as such unless they were raised by someone else.

Was Melissa and Melinda placed up for adoption? Where are their parents? Were they still alive? Were these two the only siblings, or did they have another sibling lurking in the shadows, ready to pounce? Maybe her adoptive parents had a hand in what happened to me.

So many questions I had, would they all be answered? I highly doubted it, but at this point, I didn't know what to expect. All I knew, I had to keep my guard up.

She smirked as she pointed the knife towards me.

"You should've paid more attention in science class, missy."

It took everything in me not to yell at Melinda and try to claw her eyes out. She talked about science class so casually, as if we were friends from childhood and I wasn't being held against my will.

"Why am I here?" I asked as calmly as I could.

Melinda stopped her pacing and looked at me. She stared so long with unblinking eyes that I thought she had frozen.

"Revenge."

The word rolled off her tongue so effortlessly, yet it sliced through my chest so painfully. Her cutting me with that knife would've hurt less.

"Revenge? For what? I didn't do anything wrong."

"Please." She gave me a pointed look. "Drop the bullshit. You're the reason my sister is locked behind bars."

Melinda and Melissa were both delusional. How in the hell did she think I was responsible for Melissa going to prison? Melissa pulled the trigger that killed Candace right after our sushi date. I just so happened to be there to witness it.

"I didn't…"

"Yeah, I know."

Her nostrils flared as she stared with intent.

"You're the type to play innocent when you're guilty, but that doesn't fly with me."

Yeah, it was time to keep my mouth shut. The safest thing I could do was listen. I'd only respond when specifically asked a question. I had to go about this the smart way.

"I'm here to do the job that my sister's husband miserably failed to do."

Oh boy. She was out for blood.

"Especially after all he has put her through."

Did Trevor do more to Melissa than I had already known? Was Candace not the first relationship he had behind Melissa's back? Was there more to the story?

"Melissa is my baby sister," she began as she walked back and forth in front of me. "I was born seven minutes before she was. It's my job to protect her at all costs."

Who did Melissa need protection from? In my opinion, she didn't need any protection. She was the reason she sat in prison, ordering Melinda around to do her dirty work for her.

"Did Melissa put you up to this?"

I knew I was better off not saying anything, but I couldn't help myself. I had to know who came up with the plan. Not that it really mattered, they were both crazy.

"She might've mentioned the idea to me once she was behind bars for six months."

Wow. Melinda was Melissa's puppet. How could she drag her sister down the path of destruction? She should know, regardless of how things ended with me, her sister would go down for what she'd done. She might be successful at getting rid of me, but she can't get rid of the law.

"My plan was already in motion the day Melissa was sentenced, though."

She shrugged and chuckled.

"I guess we truly think alike." She paused as she tapped her chin with her index finger. "It's almost like we're the same person."

Yeah, she got that right. The same lunatic with the same goal in mind. Get rid of the only witness to a crime Melissa decided to commit.

"I didn't know Melissa had a sister, let alone a twin sister," I commented.

Thinking back to the day Melissa was sentenced, I didn't recall seeing anyone in the courtroom with her face.

"Did you go to her sentencing?"

Asking that question might've been risky, but I couldn't help myself. I had to know.

"No."

She shook her head before she lowered her eyes to the ground. She stopped pacing and looked at me.

"I couldn't stand to see Melissa sentenced and dragged out of there in shackles for a crime that I feel should've been justified, considering the circumstance." Taking a deep breath, she exhaled. "That bitch got what she deserved."

Straight dagger to the heart.

It took every fiber of my being not to react and pummel Melinda to a pulp. If she didn't have that knife, I would've struck her. Candace didn't deserve to be talked down in such a manner. She might not have made the best decisions, but she was an amazing woman. Yes, Candace had some fault in the affair that took place. Melissa was mad at the wrong person, though. It was Trevor who committed to Melissa that he would be faithful to her. She should've been mad at Trevor instead of Candace. She didn't deserve to be talked down by the likes of her.

"She's truly my rock. We've been through a lot together. We were young when our birth parents gave us up. We were adopted by an amazing, loving family, but they were killed five years ago in a car accident."

Man, I felt for them. Considering I was being held hostage by one sister and the other sister had already tried to kill me, one might think I shouldn't. It was hard not to, though. Out of us all, I actually had a heart.

"I'm sorry to hear about your loss."

"Thank you." Melinda's eyes flicked to the ground. "They were amazing people."

After exhaling, Melinda slapped her face with her left hand.

"Snap out of it, Melinda. Don't get soft on me now."

My mouth dropped open as I watched the scene before me. Melinda was unhinged and crazy. If I wasn't sure of it before, after watching her slap herself, I knew it then.

"Do you have any more siblings?"

It was important to get as much information out of her as I possibly could. The more I knew, the more I could relay once I could break free from this hellhole.

"Yes, actually. Our older brother's name is Michael."

Melissa, Melinda, and Michael?

Melinda smiled as she tucked her hair behind her ear. "Yeah, our parents had a thing for M names. Boy, were we close."

Melinda looked at the knife before she stuffed it back in her hoodie.

"Did you stop being close when your adoptive parents passed away?"

Melinda bit the corner of her lip as she shook her head. "We stopped being close when he decided not to help me torture you."

My heart dropped into the pit of my stomach. At least one of the siblings was sane.

"He thought Melissa shouldn't have killed that bitch, but what does he know?"

Exhaling, I looked away from Melinda. For her to talk down about someone she didn't even know was beyond me. She was doing everything in her power to defend her sister, though. She had a ride-or-die mentality.

"So, you're doing all of this by yourself?"

Melinda nodded.

"Aren't I a genius?" She was quiet for a

moment. "An evil genius?"

Giving off a nervous laugh, I looked around the area once again in search of a weapon. All I needed was a pipe or a stick.

"You can stop looking for a weapon. I'm not dumb enough to leave you anything you can hurt me with here, silly."

"If you had no help, how did you get me here?" I looked around in disgust. "Wherever this is?"

"A lot of strength." Melinda chuckled. "Getting you into my car was the worst part, but I managed to maneuver you inside." She panted her arm. "Lifting those weights really benefited me."

The tension in the room was so thick I could slick it with the knife that Melinda hid in her hoodie pocket.

"Anyways, I can't stand visiting Melissa once a week while an officer supervises our visits. That's not the life I envisioned for us."

"Doing this won't help Melissa get out of prison." I motioned my hands around the cage. "The only thing this is going to do is place you behind bars right along with her."

Melinda raised an eyebrow as she crossed her arms across her chest.

"Do you really think that?"

Was that a trick question? If I answered yes, Melinda might harm me right now. If I answered no, she'd think I was a wimp, too scared to back what I originally said. Either way, I answered, I wouldn't win.

"That's what I thought," Melinda said, taking my silence as an answer.

"I've done my time behind bars, and it's not fair for my sister to be there. In the end, I want your husband to suffer just as much as I have suffered."

Narrowing my eyes at Melinda, my hands turned clammy. Melinda had done time behind bars. For what, though? Was it a simple crime? Was it more complex, something I should worry about?

"You want to keep me locked up down here to torture Zach?"

Melinda shook her head.

"No, I want to lure Zach down here when it's the right time so he can watch me kill you."

The room. Was it spinning? Was it growing smaller?

Melinda was even more cruel than Melissa. Absolutely nothing could justify the evil they held within themselves.

"Zach has nothing to do with this." Anger bubbled within me. "I was the one who witnessed my best friend dying in front of me. I was the one who testified against your sister."

Looking up towards the ceiling, I willed tears not to appear, but my emotions had a mind of their own. How was I angry one second and crying the next?

"I don't care." Melinda shrugged. "If Melissa suffers, everyone will suffer."

Melinda pulled her knife out once more.

Opening my mouth to say something, Melinda interrupted me with a wave of her knife.

"I'm done listening to you talk. If I hear anything else from you, I might snap."

With a roll of her eyes, she spun around and walked to the gate.

My feet stayed glued to the ground where I stood with my mouth wide open. The mood changes were nothing like I had imagined when she first walked down here.

After she opened the gate and closed it back behind her, she lifted the hoodie and placed it back over her head.

"You stink," she said before she turned her back and disappeared upstairs.

Chapter Twenty

Zach

Staring at Melinda's face, I threw my hand over my mouth. My eyes widened and my stomach churned.

"Zach, tell me, who is it?"

Melissa and Melinda were twins. Not only were they twins, but they were also identical. Down to the mole on the right side of their face.

"It's Melissa's twin. Her name is Melinda."

"What?" Jake yelled. "How in the hell does

she have a twin? Did you know this?"

"Hell no, I didn't know," I answered, matching Jake's energy. "

I knew Melissa wouldn't have told me about a twin, but I thought Trevor would've. He held a key piece of information from me, and it severely slowed down my investigation. If he had informed me of this when I visited him weeks ago, I would've already had Destiny home with me.

If given the chance, I would wring his neck once I saw him again, regardless of whether a police person was around or not. I'd quickly forget that I was employed by law enforcement.

"So, does this mean Melinda is behind Destiny's disappearance?"

I was 99.99 percent sure that Melinda was responsible for Destiny's disappearance.

Granted, she and Destiny were the same size, so I wasn't sure how she would have gotten her into her car if Destiny fought, which I was sure she did, or she knocked her unconscious before attempting to put her inside.

"It's possible, but all the evidence I currently have is circumstantial."

"Circumstantial?"

"Melissa's implied she might know who's responsible for Destiny's disappearance. She didn't directly come out and say it."

"Do you think her twin is responsible for everything?"

"I don't know," I admitted.

There were two things I wasn't sure about.

Did Melinda have help from someone else on the outside? Who was the mastermind behind this devious plan?

Melissa could've talked Melinda into her devious plan... or it could've been the other way around. Something told me that Melissa might've been the mastermind. She was able to talk Trevor, a former officer, into helping her. If she could talk him into doing that, she could manipulate anyone into helping her.

Or Melinda could've wanted revenge for her sister and did it all herself.

Either way, it was impossible for Melissa not to be aware of what was going on. Even though she was behind bars, she was more involved in what took place on the outside than she led on.

Clicking into my email, the secure email had arrived two minutes ago.

"I have Melissa's phone records and visitor's log to go through. Hopefully, after I review all this information, we will know more about who was responsible."

"Thank you for keeping me updated."

After hanging up the phone, I clicked on the email and went through everything, piece by piece.

Racking my brain, I tried to remember seeing Melinda during Melissa's sentencing, but I didn't remember seeing her. That was one face I would've been able to pick out of a crowd of people. Either she was there and stayed in the shadows, or she didn't come to the sentencing at all. I would've remembered seeing her.

After going through two years' worth of visitor's logs, I learned that Melinda visited Melissa once a week. Michael only came to visit around the holidays. She had some other visitors, but the visits were very sporadic. According to the visitors log, Melinda is the only one who stayed faithful to her visits to see Melissa.

Diving into the phone records, I gasped when I saw there were a ton of manuscripts and audio clips for me to wade through. There were over two hundred calls, and from the looks of things, the majority of them came from Melinda.

Going to the phone calls two days before Destiny went missing, I quickly scanned through the manuscripts, searching for specific words. The word package caught my attention, and I went back to read that response in its entirety.

Melissa: When are you going to pick up that package?

Melinda: I'm going Friday night. I will have to track the package before I can pick it up though. Don't you worry, I won't disappoint you little sis.

Melissa: Okay, big sis. I know I can always count on you.

Package? They referred to Destiny in code. There was no doubt in my mind. What other 'package' could they refer to? Destiny was kidnapped Friday night. Melinda went to pick up the package Friday night.

Grabbing my computer and folder, I walked

into the dining room and grabbed a notepad. Scribbling my thoughts, I read another conversation two days later.

On Friday night, a few minutes past eight o'clock, a call was made to Melinda.

Melissa: Did you take care of that package?

Melinda: Yes, I did. It's in the trunk as we speak.

Melissa: Did you have a problem placing the package in the trunk?

Melinda: It was a struggle, but I managed to do it.

Melissa: If only Michael would've helped you, it would've been easier on you.

Melinda: Michael doesn't want to help us. Honestly, I don't think he cares. He made that very clear when I called and asked for his assistance.

Melissa: We don't need him. We have each other, that's all that matters. I just wish he thought like us. Can I ask you something?

Melinda: You can ask me anything.

Melissa: What would I do without you?

Melinda: Trust me, I wouldn't be me without you. I love you.

Melissa: I love you too.

Melinda: I'll be in touch.

Melinda stuffed my wife into a freaking trunk? What the hell was wrong with her? Was Destiny awake and tied up while they traveled to God knew where? Was she in fear for her life, not knowing what would happen next? Or was she knocked out by some type of substance?

The following day, a call was made to Melinda.

Melissa: How's our package?

Melinda: It's resting in the basement.

Destiny was somewhere that had a basement. Where though? Some surrounding cities had basements. I just had to find out which ones.

Melissa: Do you remember the plan?

Melinda: Yes Melissa, I do. Partly because I'm the mastermind behind it.

Melinda came up with the idea to kidnap Destiny. Surprisingly, I thought she would prove to me she was the one behind this devious plan.

Melissa: Hey, you can't take all the credit here.

Melinda: I promise, I won't disappoint you. The plan is in motion.

Three days later, another call was recorded.

Melissa: How is the package?

Melinda: Very fragile to say the least.

Melissa: Oh, that's what I like to hear.

Rolling my eyes in disgust, I continued reading.

Melinda: This is coming together so perfectly.

Melissa: It's safe to say, for the first time in a while, I feel like everything is coming together.

Melinda: I'm doing everything in my

power to make sure it does.

Scrolling down, I skipped all the normal conversations that should be had daily. Sadly, I wasn't dealing with normal people.

My scrolling came to a halt days later.

Melinda: I just made that call.

Immediately, I stopped reading and grabbed my phone. Quickly comparing the date on the manuscript and the date that I received the call from the blocked number, I slowly exhaled. The calls were made on the same day. This was the nail in the coffin I needed to continue my search into Melinda.

Melissa: You did? How did it go?

Melinda: Feathers were definitely ruffled. I would say score for the Armstrong girls.

Score? Forcing my wife to call me and tell me she was scared out of her mind was a score to them?

Melissa: Sis, you make me so proud.

Melinda: I try my best, you know that.

Melissa: We have them right where we want them. It's time to suffer.

Melinda: That's exactly what I plan to happen.

Balling my hands into fists, I closed out the manuscript and my emails. I didn't need any more information from it. I had all the information I needed from it, and now it was time to find more information on Melinda.

Immediately, I went into my work database and plugged all her information in. Almost instantly, arrest records for Melinda came back.

Clicking into the most recent one, I stared at Melinda's devilish smile. Her hair was disheveled. She was booked for criminal harassment, but she only received a misdemeanor. She did six months behind bars before she was released to do six months of probation. Surprisingly, she did her probation with no hiccups.

The first arrest was made five years prior. Gasping at the information I read, I looked away from the screen in disbelief.

Did I really just read what I thought I just read?

Taking another look at the computer screen, the information didn't change.

Melissa was charged with vehicular manslaughter when her adoptive parents were killed. She was driving when she ran through a red light, and an SUV smacked the vehicle in the side where her parents were sitting, killing them instantly.

She spent two months in an asylum before she was transferred to jail for the remainder of her one-year sentence.

The more I dug into their family information, the more scandalous information I uncovered.

Now, I had to find out if there was any property within a few hours' radius that she had in her name or anyone else's name that was closely connected to her.

Once I entered Melinda's name into a separate database, her name popped up for a white SUV registered under her name.

Jotting down the tag number on my phone, I clicked on the other result of my search. Her name came back on a house with a man named Gabriel Hendricks.

Gabriel and Melinda married and divorced within three years. While they were married, they purchased a home together in Elk Grove. Taking a glance at the address, I noticed that the street didn't ring any bells.

After pulling the address up, everything came together slowly.

The house they purchased together was located on the outskirts of the city, practically in the middle of nowhere.

Grabbing the computer's screen, I planted my face against the screen.

From the outside, the house looked so ragged. I just hoped, if Destiny was inside, it looked better in there than it did on the outside. My hope slowly dwindled as I clicked through the images.

The place was a fixer-upper that was in horrible shape. Destiny, of all people, didn't deserve to be in such a shit hole. She deserved much more, like a three-bedroom home in the neighborhood of her choice.

When I came across an image of the basement, I almost passed out.

I had to go get Destiny, and I had to do it now. This was the one and only lead I had to go off of, and I thought it was a damn good one. I had to get to this house and clear it. On the one hand, I wanted Destiny there so I could rescue her. On the other hand, I yearned for her to be held hostage somewhere decent.

In due time, I would know exactly what happened. Thirty minutes or less.

My truck roared to life, and I flew out of my neighborhood at record speed once I placed Melinda's address into my GPS.

Should I call Frank and let him know I finally uncovered exactly what I thought in the first place? Or should I wait until I arrive at the scene to do the call?

I was ninety-eight percent sure Destiny was held in that house. It was the other two percent that hung in the air with uncertainty. With how devious Melissa and Melinda were, would Melinda really hold Destiny in a house with her name attached to it?

It was hard to think like a criminal, but I was in the field where I had to do it often.

If I were a seasoned criminal, I would find an abandoned place in the middle of nowhere to hold the person I kidnapped hostage.

I wouldn't take them anywhere that connected to me because anything and everything could be tracked down in law enforcement. That would take more time and effort to accomplish. Melinda didn't seem like a seasoned criminal. She was an amateur at best. I had to give her props, though. She kept me on my toes so well that I forgot to look into key things that would've led me to Destiny quicker. From what I read in the manuscript, Destiny should still be alive. They said 'them' when they talked about suffering. That only meant they wanted Destiny and me to suffer before everything went to hell.

Hopefully, I'd intercept before anything drastic happened.

Once I entered Elk Grove, I exited the highway and made a beeline for the house. The house was only two minutes from the highway, in the middle of nowhere. I'd have to play it safe.

I'd have to park down the road, out of sight. I didn't want Melinda to see my vehicle, get spooked, and act out of fear.

Pulling off on the shoulder, I pulled farther off the road before I killed the ignition.

Pulling my gun from the glove compartment, I placed it in my holster. Stepping out of the truck, I looked around at the surrounding bushes, trees, and fauna.

I needed to head east a quarter of a mile before I'd arrive at the house.

Pushing branches, leaves, and brush out of the way, I maneuvered through the woods with purpose. Reptiles scurried in front of me as I trudged through the woods.

When I came to an opening, I saw a white SUV parked in front of the same old, rugged-looking house I saw online. Wooden boards covered every window on the house.

Opening my phone, I compared the tag numbers for her vehicle, and they were a match.

Melinda was there. The real question was, was Destiny there?

Immediately, I dialed Frank. Answering on the second ring, he called out, "I have some important news to share with you."

Whoa, right to the jump. No hello, no nothing. The news must've been great.

"What news?"

Pushing a tree branch out of my view, I got a better look at the house.

"We believe we know where Destiny is," he called out.

"Yeah, I believe I know where she is as well. Bring back up to Melissa Armstrong's house in Elk Grove."

"How did you find out…"

"I have to go get my wife," I finished for him.

"You can't go in there by yourself. It's too dangerous."

Giving off a sarcastic laugh, I shook my head in disgust. "It's too dangerous for my wife to stay in there another second. She's been stuck in there long enough."

"Wait for backup. I have local police en route to the area right now. They should be there in five or ten minutes."

"Yeah, okay."

Frank was in the middle of speaking when I hung up on him.

Wait for backup, my ass. It was time to go get Destiny. I'd give my life for her. There was no way I'd wait for backup.

Grabbing my gun out of its holster, I pushed out of the woods and ran across the overgrown lawn. Leaning my back against the south side of the house, I looked around the corner towards the front of the house. Tiptoeing to the front door, I pressed my ear against it. I couldn't hear anything.

Touching the doorknob, I was surprised when it turned.

Why would she leave the door unlocked? Was this a setup? Did she know I was on my way? Did she have any way to know that information?

Whatever the reason, I didn't have time to think about it. It was time to get Destiny… or die while trying.

Chapter Twenty-One

Destiny

"Destiny."

Fluttering my eyes open, I looked around. Darkness no longer lingered. I relaxed outside on a lounge chair, and the sun shone brightly in the sky, giving off the perfect amount of warmth. Looking at the person beside me, I gasped.

"Candace."

She sat beside me, sipping on a pina colada with her legs kicked up. Her pink toenails glistened in the sun.

Candace lifted her sunglasses from her eyes, revealing her beautiful eyes. She raised her eyebrow and looked at me.

"Are you okay?" she asked me.

Concern was etched in her facial expression.

"How are you here right now?"

I could've sworn she was violently taken from me two years ago. Yet there she was in my presence, very much alive.

Her pineapple scent shampoo wafted towards me, making me feel at home. Boy, I missed that scent.

"Don't you remember?" She chuckled as she lowered her sunglasses over her eyes.

I stared at her, not knowing what answer she expected.

"I requested today off from work so we could hang out," she responded when she realized I wouldn't reply.

She did? Why didn't I remember that? What was wrong with me?

"I think you need to lay off the alcohol." She pointed at my drink in my hand. "Or relax your mind a bit. It's summer vacation, for goodness sake."

It's summer? I swore it was just spring, right?

"Yeah, you're right," I answered before I sipped my drink.

The last thing I wanted was for Candace to think I was crazy.

I needed to relax. Being at the beach today, I

needed to let loose.

Candace whistled as she lifted her sunglasses again.

"Do you see that cutie over there?"

She pointed off in the distance at a man with a mass of curls on his head. He talked to two other men animatedly, moving his hands before he laughed.

"Yeah," I answered.

"You think he's single?"

Analyzing his nice build and muscular stature, I answered, "If a guy that cute is single, he's probably a player."

Candace smiled and winked at me before she ran her fingers through her curls.

"I doubt he's a bigger player than I could ever be."

"Candace?" I gasped. "A player? No way."

Candace could be in love with a man one day and completely despise him the next.

Candace sat her drink down and stood before she looked at me.

"How do I look?"

Candace spun around in a circle before she struck a pose, flaunting her flawless body in her pink bikini.

"Stunning," I complimented her.

"Thank you. Watch and learn how to properly snag a man's attention."

"Yeah, I'll watch and learn. As if I care to snag someone's attention."

"One day, you will. I promise."

Candace headed in the direction of the men when a noise came from afar.

What was that? Shielding my eyes, I looked up into the sky, but I didn't see anything out of the ordinary. Turning around in my chair, there was no one in close range of me.

The noise sounded again, and everything gradually dimmed.

"Candace," I yelled.

As soon as Candace turned around, everything went black.

Throwing my eyes open, I stared into the darkness.

Candace.

Finally, my recurring dreams finally made sense. The last two were a jumble of mixed, false information with a little bit of truth. This last one actually happened just like that, without the confusion of time on my part.

Was Candace making contact with me? Was I being prepared for the afterlife on my way out of this world? Was I on my way to see Candace again? I wanted to see Candace, but I wasn't ready to go where she was right now.

Another noise from above startled me, sending my heartbeat into a frenzy. Staring up at the ceiling, I waited for another sound.

What was Melinda doing upstairs? Was she preparing her attack on me? Was this my last few moments of being alive?

I wasn't ready to leave my parents or my mother-in-law. Mom and Robert had been there for me since I was little, and Dennis had only been in my life two-and-a-half years.

I wasn't prepared to leave my friends. They made life after losing Candace bearable. Life in limbo, between Candace's death and our friendship developing and blossoming, was a horrible time for me. I didn't know who I was anymore, and they made me see who I was. An amazing friend who was caught in the crossfires of a love triangle that I wasn't aware of.

I wasn't prepared to leave Zach. For goodness sake, we had just married not even a month before I was kidnapped.

Our lives were placed on hold, all because Melissa and Melinda couldn't control their anger, and the hand of revenge held a tight grip on them.

We were in the middle of searching for our dream home when Melinda snatched me out of my world to put me in a metal hellhole. The school year was ending, and at this rate, I might never see my second graders ready themselves for third grade. We might never have the opportunity to adopt the dog we desire. My parents might not ever see me alive again, and that didn't sit well with my soul. No parent should ever have to bury their child.

Zach and I had so much more to live and do with each other before it was our time to leave this world. Before it was my time to leave.

The door opened, and a line of light shone in for a few moments before the door closed. The light disappeared, and I was surrounded by darkness all over again.

It was time to fight. I had no choice but to take my chance right then at that moment. How Melinda talked when she came down there two days ago made me truly understand how unhinged she truly was. The only way to handle an unhinged individual was to catch them off guard, surprising them when they least expected it.

Turning onto my side, I faced the gate, closed my eyes tight, and relaxed my body so it wasn't tense.

Footsteps sounded on the stairs. Footsteps ceased, bringing an eerily silence to the area. When satisfied with what she saw, keys jingled in the door. Slowly opening an eye, I watched her walk in. She wore a t-shirt and a pair of distressed jeans. She had no reason to wear the jacket or the face mask anymore since she revealed her identity to me. She carried a tray of food and water. She lowered herself to the foot of my bed and sat the tray down.

It was now... or never. I probably would never get another chance like this ever again. I mustered every ounce of strength I had within me and fought for my life.

Springing off the bed, I charged at Melinda as I screeched at the top of my lungs.

With my arms extended in front of me, I pushed her as hard as I could. She fell against the cage, making the metal rattle.

A look of disbelief washed over her face as

she realized her mistake. She dropped her guard when she got too comfortable, believing I was asleep, and it came to bite her in the ass.

She stared at me with a death stare that could kill a nation.

Turning on my heel, I ran towards the open door.

"You bitch," she yelled.

If time was on my side, I'd have time to slam the door on Melinda and lock her in her own cage, but when I looked over my shoulder, she was on my heels.

That wasn't good. Not at all.

Before I could make it to the first step of the stairs, Melinda wrapped her arms around my shoulders. Her hold restricted any movements that would advance me forward.

With no other choice, I had to activate what Zach taught me over the years.

Lowering my body, I jerked my right elbow into Melinda's chest. She shrieked, loosening her grip on me. With one more switch jerk of my elbow, Melinda let go of me.

It took everything in me to use my arms and legs to climb the stairs. Melinda hadn't been feeding me enough, and I truly felt how weak I was now since I was forced to use all the energy I had stored.

This woman was too smart for her own good. She had to be stopped, whether she liked it or not. I just hoped I had it in me to stop her.

Once I was on the landing, I didn't have

enough time to catch my breath before I threw the door open. With my only choice being to head to the left, I ran with caution.

I had only seen Melinda while being there, but that didn't mean she didn't have an accomplice who helped in the background. Hell, for all I knew, they could lie in wait, waiting to react at the perfect moment. I couldn't let that put fear in my bones. There was no going back. It was all or nothing now.

When the floor opened out, I realized I was in the kitchen and dining room.

Before I could even think of looking in drawers for a knife, my hair was grabbed, and my head was yanked backward.

Staring into Melinda's crazed face, her face raged with red. She was pissed, but there was no way she was more pissed than me.

"Where do you think you're going?" she seethed.

Pain resonated from my head, the force from her pull too intense. When I didn't respond, she pulled tighter on my hair.

"I've been too damn nice to you. Now, I'm going to torture you. You're not going anywhere."

"I'm getting out of here," I responded before I balled my hands into fists and swung them with all my might.

She yelled out in pain as she released my head and grabbed her mouth.

"You made me bleed."

Removing her hands from her mouth, blood

leaked out of her mouth and dripped onto her lips, leading a trail to her chin.

"You're dead, bitch."

She ran over to the drawer closest to the refrigerator, opened it up, and pulled out the biggest knife I had ever seen in my life.

At that moment, I realized I made a huge mistake. I hadn't planned my escape correctly.

As time seemed to move in slow motion, the only thing that I could think to do was run. I didn't know where I was running to, but it was my only option. My only choice.

No matter how much training Zach had done with me, one thing he told me repeatedly was, "You can be the best fighter in this world, but it is nearly impossible to win a fight with someone who has a weapon."

Whenever my body was found, I wanted Zach to know I put up the biggest fight I could muster. I didn't go out of this world willingly. I fought to the end. I hoped he would be proud of me once he was able to get through his grief of losing his wife, who he married a month ago. Had it been a month? It felt like years since I'd seen him, my family and my friends.

The time Zach and I shared together was unimaginable. I was glad to experience love like that before leaving this world.

Now, I would be able to see Candace again. For her to be killed by one twin and for me to be killed by the other didn't sit well with me. I could see the headline now. 'Best friends killed by twin sisters two-in-a-half years apart'.

Running out of the room, my breath escaped me when I saw the barrel of a gun pointed at me.

"Destiny," a familiar voice called out.

Coming to a complete stop, my eyes landed on the most beautiful man I had ever seen.

I couldn't believe my eyes. Was I dreaming? Was I already dead?

"Zach," I choked out.

Chapter Twenty-Two

Zach

Destiny ran into the living room with fear in her eyes. She wore the same outfit she had on when she left to go to Emma's house to hang out with the ladies. The only difference was that her outfit was now dirty, stained with filth. Her hair was still in a messy bun, but now her hair was matted.

When she looked in my direction, her hands went up, trembling.

"Destiny."

Didn't she recognize me?

Her eyes moved away from the gun and found my eyes. Recognition, love, and relief flashed in them.

"Zach."

She looked like she had gone through hell these past three weeks. Her eyes were swollen and puffy. Her lips were dry and cracked, but she was the most beautiful woman I had ever laid eyes on. I couldn't believe she stood in front of me.

The door behind Destiny swung open. A knife-wielding Melinda came out, a crazed look in her eyes. Blood dripped down her chin. Destiny's eyes widened, and she ran behind me.

"Melinda, drop the knife and put your hands up."

She came to a stop, snickering as she looked from me to Destiny. She lowered her hand, but she didn't drop the knife.

"Melinda, drop the knife and put your hands up. Don't make it any harder on yourself."

She tossed the knife towards my feet. She wiped the back of her hand across her chin, smearing blood on her face before she stuck her hands in the air.

Sirens echoed in the distance as I said, "Turn around, place your hands behind your back.

She rolled her eyes before she obliged. As soon as I locked the cuffs into place, four policemen ran into the house with their guns drawn.

Two walked over to Destiny, who sat on a dingy-looking couch, while the other two grabbed Melinda.

"That bitch can fight," she tossed over her shoulder as they led her towards the front door.

"I taught her well," I replied.

Turning my attention to Destiny, I rushed over to her and dropped onto the couch beside her. The couch reeked of mold and filth.

"… she told me everything," is what I heard Destiny say before I scooped her into my arms and kissed her lips.

The missing piece of my soul was finally put in place, making me whole again.

"Destiny, sweetheart, are you okay?"

She whimpered into my ear.

"I'm okay now," she replied as she ran her fingers through my hair.

The two officers walked away once I nodded that Destiny was in the best hands.

"I'm sorry it took so long for me to find out who kidnapped you."

Rubbing Destiny's back, I held onto her tight. I didn't want to let her go for fear she would disappear if I didn't have a grasp on her.

"I'm just glad you found me," she replied, a quiver in her voice.

Oh my. If Destiny cried, I wouldn't be able to hold back my own tears and emotions. I didn't want to cry in front of these policemen and Frank. Being vulnerable wasn't something I showed often, and I didn't want to show it today.

"I was so scared." She exhaled before she sniffled. "I missed you."

Hell, at this rate, I didn't care who I cried in front of. Being reunited with my wife after a horrible twenty-four days was the best feeling in the world.

Only having been married a week and having my wife taken from me was horrific. Almost three and a half weeks later, we were reunited again.

Grabbing her face, I wiped my thumbs under her eyes, catching her tears.

"I never stopped looking for you," I admitted.

Her eyes searched mine as I continued.

"I spent every moment, every hour, every minute, every damn second looking for you."

A smile touched her lips as she pressed her lips together.

"I appreciate everything you continue to do for me, but I thought you weren't supposed to help with the investigation. How did you do it?"

The front door opened, and Frank and two policemen walked in. The look on Frank's face didn't look pleasant.

"I wasn't supposed to," I admitted.

The two policemen began their rounds of the crime scene.

Destiny sighed before she gave me a pointed look.

Frank looked at Destiny and said, "Destiny, an ambulance is on its way to take you to the hospital."

Destiny looked at me, completely shocked. I

could read Destiny like the back of my hand. I knew she was shocked he hadn't even addressed me. I didn't make it any better or worse, not addressing him. If he thought I wouldn't go to the ends of the earth to locate my wife, he was mistaken and did not truly know me.

"I-I don't need medical attention." Destiny shook her head as she looked back and forth between Frank and me.

"Yes, you do need medical attention," I stated sternly.

Where was Destiny going with this? If Melinda was anything like Melissa, I knew she hadn't taken care of Destiny.

From what I could see, Destiny had lost some weight. Looking at her lips, they were cracked and close to an ash white color. It was evident she gave Destiny small amounts of food and water. She did the absolute minimum to keep her alive.

"I want to get through questioning." She looked back and forth between us. "Can we start now?"

All Destiny cared about was placing Melinda behind bars for as many years as legally possible.

Ambulance sirens sounded in the distance.

"You'll be questioned after you are looked at in the hospital," I reassured her.

Dragging my eyes up and down her body, my heart sunk into my chest. I knew she wouldn't just be looked at. She would be admitted. She had been neglected. Grabbing her hand, I gave it a squeeze.

"I promise you'll get justice for everything she has done to you."

Destiny opened her mouth to respond, but I pressed my index finger to her lips.

"I promise."

Destiny nodded before she looked at her lap.

Not even a minute later, two paramedics walked into the house.

"She's been held against her will," Frank said as he pointed at Destiny. "She needs to go the hospital."

Destiny squeezed my hand with all her might as they approached her.

"Hello, miss. Do you need a stretcher, or can you walk?"

"She needs a stretcher," I responded for her.

The paramedics went outside the door and brought the stretcher inside.

Carefully, they lifted Destiny off the couch and placed her on the stretcher.

As they strapped her to the stretcher, she said, "Please don't leave me."

She reached her hand out to me.

"I'll be right behind you," I responded as I took her hand.

Absolutely nothing would prevent me from going to be by her side.

"I love you," she called over her shoulder as I followed them out the door.

The front yard was littered with two ambulances and six cop cars.

"I love you too."

As soon as Destiny was safely placed in the ambulance, I turned around and took a step back.

Frank stood behind me with a solemn look on his face.

"We need to talk."

"Yeah, we do." I agreed. "We'll talk after I make sure my wife is fine."

Before Frank could respond, I walked away from him and made my way over to my truck.

As the siren for the ambulance started, I followed suit to the closest hospital to our location.

My wife. She was safe. She was back in my presence. No longer was she in harm's way.

Throwing my truck into park, I killed the ignition in a law enforcement's parking space.

"I'm right here," I shouted as the paramedics opened the back doors.

Destiny's face was streaked with tears, shattering my heart into a million pieces. There I was, feeling whole again, yet I knew nothing of what Destiny suffered through while she was in Melinda's care.

I thought Destiny was traumatized after what she went through two years ago, I could only imagine what this had done to her mental health.

While the paramedics wheeled Destiny into the emergency room doors, I held tight to her hand.

"Everything is going to be okay. I'm right here," I continued to reassure her.

The triage nurse stood while we approached the counter. She held a tablet in her hand.

"What is she coming in for?"

"Dehydration and malnutrition, for sure."

Looking around the emergency room, I could tell it was a busy day for them. A woman held a baby who let out a cry.

"You'll need to perform a psych evaluation after she speaks with law enforcement. She was kidnapped and held against her will."

The triage nurse looked at Destiny for a second before she typed away on her tablet.

"I'll take it from here," she said to the paramedics.

One of the paramedics shook my hand before they walked out of the emergency room.

"Hello, honey. My name is Tara. Can you tell me your first and last name?"

She sat her tablet on the counter before she placed a pulse oximeter on her finger.

"Destiny Miller."

"Well, Destiny, my job is to make sure that you are doing okay and get some vitals," she said as she typed on her tablet. "Can you tell me your birthday?"

"August second," she replied as she placed a blood cuff on Destiny's arm.

"Perfect. Now, let me take your blood pressure."

Destiny stayed still while the blood pressure cuff tightened on her arm and relaxed.

"Now, I just need to take your temperature."

She stuck the thermometer into her mouth. After a few moments, she took it out of her mouth and typed the information into the tablet.

Grabbing her phone, she made a call and said, "We need to get Destiny into a treatment room stat."

Destiny's grip on my hand tightened. Widening her eyes, she looked at Tara.

"Why stat? Is something wrong with me?" she asked.

"Calm down, Destiny. You are okay," I said into her ear.

"You are fine Ms. Miller. You are our top priority now, considering your circumstances.

Within moments, another nurse came and greeted Destiny before she led us to a small room, with two chairs and a hand-washing station.

"I'll be right back to get IV started."

Once the nurse walked out of the room, I grabbed Destiny's face and kissed her lips.

"You have no idea how much I've missed you," I said.

"I went through hell while I was in there," she admitted. Her lip quivered, and her eyes watered. "When I was there..."

"Shh," I interrupted her. "I know it's going to be hard for you to talk about it one time. I'd rather you say what happened once Frank arrives, so you don't have to continue to relive what you've been through."

"What will happen to your job?"

The last thing on my mind was my job, especially when it came to Destiny.

"Destiny, I would die for you. A job doesn't mean anything to me when your safety is at risk. So, I don't care what happens to it. If I hadn't gotten there when I did…"

I didn't even want to finish my statement. Just the thought made me want to be violently ill. What would've happened if I had gone into the house two minutes later? What would've happened if I had listened to Frank and waited for backup? I might not be sitting in the hospital next to my wife.

The nurse walked back into the room and started Destiny's IV. She squeezed my hand and squinted her eyes once the needle went into her vein.

After the nurse finished telling us that Destiny was dehydrated and malnourished, she walked out of the room to get Destiny a protein shake.

When a knock sounded on the door, I knew it was Frank. His signature announcement of his arrival was three knocks in a rhythmic manner.

"Come in," I called out.

Frank walked into the room, a notepad in hand.

"Destiny, Zach." He greeted us. "I'm here to get some information. Do you mind if we get this done now?"

"I'm ready," Destiny said eagerly.

Over the next twenty minutes, Destiny drank a protein drink while she went into detail about the horrible conditions she endured. I bit my lip the entire time of her explanation, attempting to hold back the anger that bubbled within me.

When Destiny cried, I wiped her tears with one hand while I wiped my own tears with my other hand. If I had thought Destiny was strong before, she proved to me just how strong she truly was with what she endured.

"The only thing that kept me alive was reuniting with my husband again," she finished as she squeezed my hand.

Lowering my head, I placed soft kisses on the back of her hand.

"You're a strong woman, Destiny." Frank closed his notepad and stood. "I'll be in touch if I have any other questions. Zach, we'll talk another time. Just focus on your wife."

With those parting words, Frank walked out of the emergency room.

"Is everything going to be okay?" Destiny asked me as the door closed.

I knew she referenced my job when she said everything.

"I think so," I responded.

Chapter Twenty-Three

Destiny

"You look amazing."

Tucking my freshly cut hair behind my ear, I looked at Hannah.

Twisting my mouth from side to side, I replied, "Do you really think so? I'm not sure I like it."

My haircut was on the shorter side, stopping right below my chin. I hadn't had a haircut in years, only regular trims to get rid of my dead ends.

Hannah smiled before she reached up and touched my hair.

"It compliments your face very well."

Giving myself one last glance, I closed the sun visor before I looked at Hannah.

"Thank you." Grabbing her hand, I gave it a squeeze. "What would I do without you?"

She shrugged. "Be lonely, possibly miserable," she said before she stuck her tongue out at me.

Swatting at her hand, I asked, "Are you ready for a cup of coffee?"

"I was born ready."

Opening the door to Hannah's car, I stepped outside and looked around. The sun shone high in the sky with no clouds in sight. Closing my eyes for a moment, I inhaled the fresh air and basked in the warmth on my face. Being confined inside of a basement for three and a half weeks and being hospitalized for a week right after really taught me the beauty of what I missed out on. Nature, and most importantly, freedom.

Parked two vehicles over was Zach, who stepped out of his truck. He flashed a smile, setting off a frenzy in my body.

Five days ago, I was released from the hospital. I was hospitalized for a week due to my being severely dehydrated and malnourished. I received an IV with calories during my entire stay, and I was fed nutrition-dense meals.

Once I gained a few pounds and was

hydrated, I was released. During my entire stay, Zach never left my side. He stayed with me for the entire week, even requesting a bed for him to sleep in. I knew my husband was amazing, but I never, ever expected him to stay with me 24/7 while I was in the hospital.

All my family and friends came to visit. In order not to overwhelm me with too many guests at once, Zach scheduled two visitors a day for me. I was always grateful for my family and friends, especially after Candace's death. When I stared death in the face, I was even more grateful to still be alive to see another day.

Leaving Melinda's house lifted a huge rock off my chest. I had been free for two weeks now. Not only did I suffer physically, but I also suffered mentally. I probably felt closest to death while down in that basement. My bones ached like hell from the cold temperature and the hard surface I had no choice but to sleep on. I struggled with reality when I was in seclusion. My visions, or dreams, of Candace and Zach both seemed vivid as if I could reach out and touch them. I could reach out and touch Zach. I couldn't say the same for Candace.

As Hannah and I approached the door of Meg's Coffee Shop, Zach jogged past us so he could open the door.

"What a wonderful gentleman," Hannah commented.

"Yes, gentleman, thank you."

I blew him a kiss.

He reached his hand out, grabbed it, and shoved it into his pocket.

"It's no problem," he commented as he closed the door behind us.

Meg's was busy as always, buzzing with light chatter from patrons and the occasional clink of cups from behind the counter.

Since being back, this was the first time Hannah, and I had the opportunity to get together and have some girl time. I was currently on FMLA while I dealt with my situation. On this wonderful morning, Jake, Emma, and the twins were spending quality time at a local park.

After we ordered our drinks, Zach paid for them, and we walked over to the pickup counter.

"Do you want to sit inside or outside?" Hannah asked.

Tapping my finger on my chin, I pointed outside.

"I would love the fresh air."

"I was just going to suggest that," Zach said as he slipped his hand into mine.

Beaming, I gave his hand a squeeze.

Since being out of captivity and in the hospital, I had a new outlook on life. I favored the outside as much as possible. When in the car, I'd ride with the windows down. When at home, instead of sitting in the living room for hours after work, I'd sit outside on the front porch. I'd never wish what I went through on anyone, not even my worst enemy, Melissa. Now, Melinda. Hell, I couldn't even say they were my enemy. I had never wronged them, but in their mind, they believed I had. Thankfully, they were both behind bars at different prisons, so they no longer had contact with each other.

Moments later, our drinks were sat on the counter.

Zach picked up his vanilla cappuccino and my caramel macchiato and we headed outside.

Taking a deep breath in, we walked over to the outdoor seating. Only one table was occupied. A young woman sat with her two small children in the far corner. She sipped on her drink as they chowed down on donut holes.

Hannah and I sat across from each other at one table. After Zach sat my drink down, he walked to another table a few feet away to give us some space.

"Zach treats you like a real-life goddess," she commented as she looked over her shoulder in his direction.

Looking up, Zach smiled and winked at me before he took a sip of his drink.

"Yeah, I'm a lucky woman," I agreed.

If someone had told me this would be my life, happily married to an amazing man that loved me to the ends of the earth, I wouldn't have believed them. Yet, I lived this life.

"How he treats you almost makes me want to give dating a try again. Almost."

Taking a sip of my drink, I asked, "What made you want to give up on relationships?"

"One too many horrible ones."

Hannah sipped her drink before she continued.

"After a while, I got tired of trying."

I didn't blame her. Relationships were never my thing, especially for that reason. I didn't think too much about anything long-term until Zach came into my life.

"How long ago was that?"

Hannah scrunched up her nose, deep in thought. "About three years. We met at a bar one night after midterm exams. My chemistry exam kicked my ass so hard I had to have a drink and wind down. He happened to have sat beside me and struck up a conversation."

"It sounds like the relationship started off positive. What happened that shut you off from dating?"

"Trust issues. He made the mistake of lying to me once." Hannah put her index finger up. "I found out about the lie, and the relationship dwindled from there."

"Trust is a huge attribute," I agreed. "So I can understand."

Hannah took another sip of her drink.

"You have to remember something, though," I said as the woman and her two children walked past us to leave.

She cradled her cup.

"Remember what?"

"All it takes is for the right man to come along."

Hannah raised an eyebrow. "How are you so

sure?"

Smiling, I replied, "I was the same way until Zach came into my life when I least expected to find love."

"Seriously?"

"Yeah."

I looked over at Zach as I sipped my drink. He stared at me with intent before he winked.

"He came into my life and showed me not all relationships are terrible."

Hannah smiled, a twinkle in her eyes.

"Now, don't get me wrong, it's not sunshine and rainbows all the time, but it's worth the fight."

"Maybe it's time for you to try again."

She looked off in the distance and stayed silent.

"Or at least open your mind up to the idea," I suggested.

She smiled before she said, "I think you're right."

She tapped her fingers against her cup.

"Enough about me. Let's talk about you. We haven't had the chance to sit down and talk since you've come home. How are you doing?"

"I'm doing okay."

Hannah gave me a knowing look.

"Okay? Come on, I'm one of your best friends." Hannah grabbed my hand and squeezed it gently. "You can be honest. You can tell me anything."

Pinching my lips together, I willed myself not to cry. Looking away from Hannah, I breathed in before I slowly exhaled. Deep breaths would keep me calm. Or so they should.

"It's been hard."

Hannah's eyes softened as she listened.

A tear escaped my eye, and I immediately wiped it away. Being strong wasn't always the best thing. Almost always, it was more painful to be strong 24/7. I had learned it was okay not to be okay.

"I feel like I'm in limbo," I admitted. "Like, I'm almost worse off now than I was two years ago when…"

"I know, you don't have to go into detail."

She pressed her lips together.

"I think you'll benefit from counseling again."

After sipping my drink, I said, "I started going again last week."

"Is it helping?"

Counseling started to be my aid when I was handed my first traumatic experience once everything with Candace happened. Before then, I wasn't aware of what trauma entailed. I didn't know it could keep someone up all night. I wasn't aware it could make someone into an emotionless zombie. I didn't know if it could leave you feeling empty inside. You never know until you experience it firsthand.

It took weeks for it to get better after Candace. It wasn't a quick switch that could be flipped, and I was better. It took time and effort.

This time around, I woke up more than once a night, screaming at the top of my lungs while sweat pooled on my forehead and tears wet my face from my nightmares. I did it while in the hospital and when I came back home. Every single time, Zach was right there, comforting and calming me. He'd hold my face in his hands, wiping my tears away while he told me, 'I'm right here. You are okay. No one is going to hurt you.' Since being released from the hospital, I visited my counselor three times a week.

"Yeah, it's starting to help."

Hannah beamed before she tucked her hair behind her ear.

"I'm just glad you're back. I was going crazy when you weren't here. I called Zach so many times, I'm surprised he didn't block my number."

I laughed as I looked over her shoulder.

"He wouldn't do that. He understands that you love me."

We continued to talk until both of our cups were drained of caffeine.

"It was wonderful having coffee with you today," Hannah said as we threw our trash away.

"Yeah, it was amazing."

Looking around, Zach was behind us as we walked towards the vehicles.

"Even though I'm unable to go to work, having a cup of coffee with you just makes me feel like my life is getting back on track."

"Trust me, it is."

We came to a halt at the trunk of her car.

"Text me later, okay?"

She wrapped her arms around me, and we

hugged. Boy, I missed the love and affection I received from my loved ones.

"I will, I promise."

Hannah hugged Zach next and patted him on the back.

"Take care of my best friend."

"I will, I promise."

We stood and watched Hannah back out of her parking space. As she headed towards the exit, she blew her horn, and we waved.

"Did you have a good time?"

Zach guided me to the passenger side of his truck and opened the door for me.

"I had a wonderful time," I admitted.

Zach closed the door and jogged to the driver's side.

"I'm glad you did. I know these past few days have been overwhelming, but we all love you so much."

"I love you all too."

Zach started the truck, and it roared to life. Letting down the window halfway, the sun shined in through the opening.

"Destiny, you are my life. I seriously don't know what I would've done if something would've happened to you."

Looking over, I exhaled as I watched a tear fall from Zach's eyes. Reaching over, I wiped it away and rubbed my thumb against his cheek.

"Zach, you are the reason I didn't give up. I nearly went stir-crazy in that horrible place."

Flashes danced in my eyes, and my breath

escaped me. Zach cuffed my face, bringing me back to the present.

"Mentally, I battled with myself. I knew I could've given up, and the pain I endured would go away, but I continued to think of the wonderful times we shared."

Smiling, my eyes welled with tears, but they weren't tears of sadness. They were tears of happiness.

"I didn't want to lose that, and I sure as hell didn't want to lose you. So, I fought my ass off to see you again. I refused to leave my soulmate in this world alone."

"I'm sorry I've been so protective of you since I found you. The worst days of my life were when I didn't know where you were. Now that I know you are okay, I don't want to let you out of my sight."

Pressing my forehead against his, I said, "I don't mind it at all. I love your protection. It makes me feel safe. I don't want to be left alone anytime soon."

Pressing my lips to his, my eyes fluttered close. Our mouths and tongues moved in sync while Zach cupped my face, and I grabbed a handful of his hair. A full make-out session was held in Zach's truck in Meg's parking lot. The whole world could stare in disgust if they wanted to. I learned not to ever pass up another moment, another second, minute, hour, or day. Anything could happen, and I couldn't live life without doing what I wanted to do at that moment.

When our lips separated, I opened my eyes and stared into his beautiful eyes.

"Did I mention how beautiful you are?"

Playfully rolling my eyes, I responded, "Only a million and one times."

Chapter Twenty-Four

Destiny

"How are you feeling?"

Sitting back, I crossed my left leg over my right and got comfortable on the couch. Clasping my hands together on my knees, I looked around the room.

It was painted light blue, with abstract paintings on all corners of the wall. On the far corner of the room was a modern bookshelf that contained psychology and self-help books. The constant tick of the analog clock grabbed my attention before I planted my eyes on Alice, my counselor.

She sat across from me in an ergonomic chair. Her red hair was held back by a hair clip, and she wore a black dress with a white blazer.

"I'm feeling great."

She flipped a few pages in her notepad. Pressing her glasses on top of her nose, she beamed.

"You said good the beginning of last week and okay the week before that. Did something happen that you want to discuss?"

"I've focused heavily on my exercises to calm myself."

She raised her eyebrow as she gripped her pink-inked pen.

"So, you've done your exercises more this week than in previous weeks?"

"Yes. My nightmares aren't as plentiful as they used to be."

They came on occasion, but Zach was able to snap me out of them, and I would do my breathing exercises to calm my nerves.

Scribbling on her notepad, she nodded.

"That's wonderful to hear. Since they are working so well for you, keep up those exercises."

She didn't have to tell me twice.

"I can do that."

She grabbed her cup from the coffee table beside her. She took a sip of her tea before she crossed her legs.

"I think it's safe to do your counseling session once a week instead of three times a week."

"Seriously?"

What beautiful music to my ears. To know I've made that much progress in such a short time was amazing.

"Yes, your progress is incredible. You see what can happen when you incorporate everything I teach you?"

"Yes."

I clasped my hands together.

"Amazing results."

"Is there anything else you'd like to discuss before we end our session?"

A smile peeked through, and Alice widened her eyes.

"What has you smiling like that?"

"Well..." Alice nodded.

"Yes, you can be released to go back to work."

I clapped my hands, stood up, and did a celebration dance. Even though it was summer vacation, being released to go back to work made me feel whole again. Like I took two steps in the right direction for once.

Once summer vacation ended, I'd be ready for my next class of students. I wasn't able to be there for my students to end this previous year, but if I were lucky, I wouldn't have any more hiccups headed my way.

Melissa and Trevor had been behind bars for almost three years. Those two were my first hiccups. This time around, Melinda was behind bars, and she wouldn't be getting out anytime soon. From what Melinda told me, the only person that was close to her that actually dealt with her was her brother, and he had no interest in helping her torture me. Hopefully, she was my second and final hiccup. I didn't think I had any more fight in me, but I wouldn't know for sure until I had to prepare for battle again.

Alice closed her notepad before she placed her glasses on the top of her head.

"Now, before you go off to celebrate, make sure you go to the front desk and make yourself an appointment for next week."

After saying goodbye to Alice and scheduling my next appointment, I slid my sunglasses over my eyes as I walked outside into the summer heat.

The heat this summer was no joke, and I loved every bit of it.

Once I made it to my car, I stepped inside and locked the doors. Starting the car up, I texted Zach quickly to let him know I was on the way home before I left the parking lot.

It took weeks to convince Zach to allow me to leave the house to go to counseling by myself. When I went, he would wait outside, listen to music, and scroll social media on his phone until my session ended. He went with me when it was time to go grocery shopping or fill my car up. His protectiveness made me feel warm inside, but I didn't want him to stop his life to protect me.

The last two months have had its ups and downs. Some days were so horrible that I couldn't bring myself up to get up in the morning, but my days were mostly fine. I couldn't have done it without the help of my family, friends, and counseling.

Thankfully, Zach didn't lose his job by working on my case. Several deadly silent days had passed until we had learned he was still employed with the force.

All the higher-ups who had a say in Zach's keeping his job understood his actions. They agreed that they would have done the same thing if they were in his shoes. So, to accommodate Zach, they wrote Zach up for his actions, and he could keep his job. This was Zach's first and only write-up he had received since he started his career. As Zach explained it to me, he happily smiled when he signed his write-up.

Pulling into the driveway, my heart fluttered. Zach stood in front of the front door, holding a bouquet of colorful flowers.

Before I turned my car off, Zach approached my driver's door and opened it.

"These are for you," he said as he handed me the flowers.

Taking them, I inhaled the floral scent.

"These look and smell amazing."

He took my hand and helped me out of my car.

Raising an eyebrow, I looked over my shoulder and asked, "What's going on?"

"Why does something have to be going on? Can't I just show my wife affection and gratitude?"

Beaming, I turned around and kissed him on the cheek.

"You're right."

Zach stepped in front of me and opened the front door. Immediately, the house smelled of a mixture of cleanliness and lemon.

"Did you clean?"

He nodded.

"You can never say I never got on my hands and knees and scrubbed the floors with a toothbrush."

"You did all that?" I pointed out once he closed the door and locked it.

"No, but it sounded great."

Playfully swatting at him, I walked into the living room and placed the flowers on the coffee table.

As I sat on the couch, a delightful scent drifted from the kitchen.

"Did you cook?"

"Yes, I did. Would you like to know what you'll be having for dinner?"

Clapping my hands together, I stood.

"I would love to know."

Zach had especially been more helpful around the house since my being back home.

Zach took my hand, and he led me to the dining room.

"For the lovely Mrs. Miller, I've cooked a medium rare steak with a medley of vegetables.

"Placing my hand over my chest, I admired the delicious meal Zach prepared for us.

"What did I ever do to deserve to be treated like a goddess?"

Zach pulled out a chair and guided me to it. Once I sat, he pushed me in, and he sat to the right of me.

"Exist."

Looking over at him, I waited for him to give me more than that simple, vague answer, but he said nothing.

"Shall we dig in?"

"Yes," I responded, grabbing my fork and steak knife.

After I cut a piece of steak, I forked it into my mouth. Moaning in satisfaction, my eyes rolled to the top of my head.

"Good?"

"More like amazing."

Zach smiled before silence fell upon us, and we continued eating.

"Is there anything you want to tell me?"

Stopping mid-chew, I raised an eyebrow as I sat my fork on my plate.

"Something tells me you might already."

He shrugged before he said, "Try me."

I clasped my hands together, barely holding in my excitement.

"I was released to go back to work."

He smiled so wide, all of his beautiful teeth were on display.

"That's my beautiful wife."

He reached across the table and squeezed my hand.

"Congratulations. I'm so proud of you. You've made such great progress. No matter the obstacles that have been thrown at you."

I placed my hand over my chest before the truth oozed out of me.

"I couldn't have done it without you."

Grabbing my water, I took a sip.

"Did you already know?"

He shook his head.

"I knew it was going to happen soon, but no, I wasn't sure until you told me."

Picking up my fork, I stabbed at a carrot.

"My sessions are now once a week instead of three times a week."

Zach folded his hands and placed them under his chin.

"This calls for celebration."

Motioning my hands around, I replied, "You've cleaned the house, which you've done such a fantastic job with. You've made one of my favorite meals that I can eat. What else could you possibly have up your sleeve?"

Zach winked at me before he said, "Finish your meal, and you'll find out."

Ten minutes later, our plates were clean.

After Zach insisted I give no help, he loaded the dishwasher, grabbed my hand and we walked into the bedroom.

A light floral scent floated in the air. A line of pink and red rose petals led from the bedroom door into the bathroom.

"Lead the way Mrs. Miller."

Leading the way to the bathroom, I gasped in awe.

Rose petals littered the bathroom, from the path to the vanity to the path to the bathtub. The floral scent intensified in the bathroom, giving the primary source away. Two lit candles sat on the vanity, twinkling bright.

"Romance in a shower stream?"

Zach nodded.

"I love the way you think."

Zach turned the shower on before we stripped out of our clothes. Zach slapped my butt before we stepped into the shower together.

The shower bomb in the bottom of the shower gave off the floral scent I fell in love with.

After we washed our bodies, we scrubbed each other's backs with a loofah. When it came to Zach washing my back, he did small, attentive circles before he pressed his erection against my butt.

"I want to make love to you," he whispered into my ear before he flickered his tongue against my earlobe, sending chills down my spine and all over my body.

Looking over my shoulder, I rubbed his forearms.

"Meet me in the bedroom."

Reaching out, I tried to turn the water off, but he grabbed my hand before I could.

"No."

He spun me around so I faced him.

"I want to right here."

He backed me up against the wall until my butt pressed firmly against it.

"Right now," he growled.

Before I could formulate a sentence, let alone a word, his mouth captured mine.

Hot water rained down on us, completely soaking our hair.

Tangled in each other's arms, my tongue explored his mouth with passion.

This was hot and spontaneous.

"Zach," I whispered as he raised his hand and cupped my back.

"Yes."

He moved from my mouth to my neck, placing tender, knee-bucking kisses along my sensitive spots.

"I want it rough."

Those four words had him in a tizzy. I had never spoken those words before. Honestly, I didn't even know where they came from, but I didn't want our sex to be slow and soft. Hell, I didn't want to make love. I wanted him to pound me hard and fast. I needed to feel it in every last fiber of my being.

"I'll give you just that."

He lifted my left leg, and he buried himself deep inside me.

I gasped, his intentional thrust taking my breath away. Lifting my right leg, I wrapped my legs and arms around him. Holding on for dear life, he cupped my butt and pounded me like there was no tomorrow.

Nipping at his ear, neck, and tongue only further excited me.

"I love you," I exclaimed.

"I love you too," he said as we climaxed together.

Epilogue

Destiny

Tossing the frisbee, it sliced through the air. Before it touched the ground, Baxter grabbed it with his mouth.

Baxter was the golden retriever we adopted from the humane society. Only a few days from turning ten months, he came home to a loving family after being abandoned in the parking lot of a grocery store.

Baxter trotted over to me. After grabbing the frisbee, I rubbed the top of his head before I tossed it again.

"I love watching you two play."

Glancing over my shoulder, I spied Zach sitting in the gazebo.

"It's the best feeling ever," I commented as Baxton came back over to me. "Do you want to join in?"

"No, I'm fine over here."

Tossing the frisbee once more, I shielded my eyes and watched Baxton run across our new, expansive backyard.

Zach and I found our dream home four months ago. It was a two-story, three-bedroom, two-in-a-half-bath house on four acres of land. It had all the fixtures I wanted and more, including a beautiful gazebo in the backyard. The house was more on the higher end of our budget, but it was well worth every penny we placed into it. A month ago, to the day we moved in.

After Baxton brought the frisbee back, I took it from him and fed him a treat before he trotted away.

Plopping next to Zach, I slipped my hand into his and looked off into the distance.

"What's on your mind?"

Looking over at Zach, I asked, "How do you do that?"

"I know everything about you," he said as he stared deep into my eyes. "So, what's in your mind?" he asked again.

"I'm just amazed at how everything has finally fallen into place for us."

Two months ago, Melinda went to trial. She decided to prolong the process by pleading not guilty, even though she was aware I would testify. At sentencing, she ended up with twelve years behind bars for kidnapping. Melissa was also sentenced to another five years for her part in the mastermind of the crime. In the end, we learned that Trevor had absolutely nothing to do with what happened to me. He was cleared of all wrongdoings, and Zach respected him for that.

"Yes, it's a beautiful thing. I have my wonderful wife next to me." He lightly squeezed my hand. "We have our sweet Baxter over there." He pointed across the yard. "I have everything I want and more."

Beaming, I cupped his face and kissed him. "I love you forever, Zachary Miller."

"I love you more, Destiny Miller."

Stay tuned for my next book that will be coming out. It is currently in the writing/editing process and it will be available in the near future. I cannot wait for you to read it!

OTHER TITLES BY ANA DENISE

His Crazy Obsession Series

His Crazy Obsession

His Unstable Obsession

Dangers in Love Series

Dangers in Love

SIGN UP FOR MY AUTHOR NEWSLETTER

Be the first to learn about Ana Denise's new releases and receive exclusive content!

www.authoranadenise.com

Thank you for reading!

Please add a review on Amazon and let me know what you thought!

Amazon reviews are extremely helpful for authors, thank you for taking the time to support me and my work. Don't forget to share your review on social media and with hashtag #LostinLove and encourage others to read the story too!

Ana Denise was born and raised on the Treasure Coast of Florida in 1999. She considers her family and friends to be most significant in her life. Growing up, she has always been fascinated with reading and writing short stories. Following her passion, she has decided to become a romance author after obtaining a Bachelor's Degree in Business Administration.